The Unwanted Bride

Book 7
(The Viking Serie

By
Marti Talbott
© 2018

In a village situated in the forest, and out of sight of the well-traveled road, lived two sisters, Jinny and Owena Allaway, the eldest of which was Owena. Pleasing to look upon, Owena was never without the attentions of men, while Jinny was ignored and often left wanting. Yet, Jinny loved her sister and wished all manner of happiness for her. At least that's what she always thought. It was not until two MacGreagor brothers came to choose brides that her devotion was put to the ultimate test.

CHAPTER 1

THERE CAME UPON THE land of Scotland a terrible drought.

Situated on a plateau above the base of the northern mountains, the once thriving MacGreagor villagers found themselves surrounded by a suffering few had ever seen before. Normally they feared too much rain, for such would rot their vegetable gardens and the crops in the lowlands, leaving them with little to eat. The reverse was completely unthinkable.

A storm would come - it always had before.

Just in case, they kept watch, using a stick to measure the water level in the river that ran alongside the village. When a week passed and then two and it still had not rained, they began to store water in as many vessels as they could find. Mountain streams that fed the nearby river, became little more than a trickle, and then flowed no more. Far too soon, the once raging river yielded only a muddy bottom, as the blistering summer sun dried even that.

The MacGreagors stayed home, even though they knew their daily circumstances diminished their chances of survival. Day after day, no storm clouds gathered and the wind brought only more dry heat. In the glens below the mountains, the once bluish green rolling hills, became just as brown and uninhabitable as their own land. Clansmen, who often rode from village to village carrying the news, came far less often. Even then, they were convinced that when the rain returned, those in the mountains would reap the rewards first. All they needed to do was wait. As well, leaving their home, the place of their births, seemed impossible. Surely the drought would soon end. It was Scotland, after all.

They were wrong.

The time finally came when they were forced to set the livestock free to wander where they may in search of food and drink. Most went into the forest where some small measure of green grass remained, others disappeared completely. It was, after all, more important to save what water they had for the people. And die, the sheep, cows and horses did, suffering a cruel, unquenchable thirst until death overcame the weak and then the strong. The wolves, wildcats and red foxes came down out of the mountains to feast on carcasses the MacGreagors had not the strength nor inclination to bury, making it dangerous for the people to leave their cottages without men with weapons to protect them.

The elders, having given their ration of what little water, mead and wine was left to the young, died and with them went many of the stories of their heritage. They were the sons and daughters of Vikings, but it mattered not, for too urgent was the need for water.

At first, vague reports in the lowlands held that there was an abundance of water in England, but later reports claimed the English were dying in even greater numbers than the Scots. For the MacGreagors in the far north, England lay half a world away, yet with great reluctance, three MacGreagor men thought to take their chances. They gathered their families, all that they could carry, and whistled for their horses. Only four horses heard the call and responded.

One man among the three was Bearnard MacGreagor. At not yet seventeen, Bearnard married fourteen-year-old Edana, the girl he had loved since they were children. He expected their future to be one of good health and fortune, the same as all those who lived in the village before him, but it was not to be. On that fateful day, he lifted his wife up, set her on his horse and with a heavy heart, left those few

MacGreagors remaining, family one and all, and followed the others down the path that would take them to the lowlands.

Finding that their neighbors in the lowlands were put upon to dig wells to quench their own thirst, and had little to spare, the future of those three families looked bleak indeed. Their neighbor's generosity allowed the men to fill but one flask each with water, and gave the already thirsty horses a few lifesaving swallows. It was enough – it had to be, and the MacGreagors were more than grateful.

Not knowing in which direction water could truly be had, it was decided that to insure the survival of at least one part of the clan, the MacGreagors would separate, one family going west toward the Irish Sea, one east toward the North Sea, and the third hoping to make it to the great river in the south.

Bearnard said a last goodbye to his kinfolk, and set about to see if he could find water between the main road that led south to England, and the Irish Sea. It was the same grim looking abandoned land they could see from their mountain plateau, and just as he expected, the way was long, and the ground hard and dusty. Yet, Bearnard said little as he walked beside the horse, kept watch over his wife's health and stayed alert should they be attacked by wild animals.

Aside from his weapons, he carried with him a hatchet, his only other shirt, seed for planting, a flint rock and a small, crude piece of steel with which to start fires. On his body, he wore an unbearably hot bearskin cloak, handed down from generation to generation, yet necessary to see them through should they have to endure a harsh winter. He also had on long pants, a tunic that hung just above his knees, his wide belt, his sword, his bow, a sheath of arrows, and three small diamonds gained from the necklace of a woman he never knew. As well, Edana carried all she could including their blanket, extra clothing, and several small flasks filled with the spices necessary to make their food palatable.

More often than not, his clothing caught on the dry, thorny bushes. Instead of determining their way, he allowed the horse to take them where it would, for everyone knew that if there was water to be had, the horse would find it. For the most part, they followed well-trodden animal paths, and Bearnard complained not, even when the paths took them more south than west.

Exhausted by the time the sun set each night, they slept under the light of a billion stars, the breathtaking beauty of which seemed somehow cruel considering their circumstances. Come a new morning, they set out again. The sun dried their parched lips, long and wide stretches with few trees brought them no relief, and for his wife's sake, Bearnard stopped to rest more often than would have been necessary on a normal journey.

On the third day, a slight breeze gave them hope, and they eagerly searched the sky for some hint of dark clouds on the horizon. It was not to be – not that day and not in the days that followed. Yet, there were hills ahead that possibly hid from them mountains from which all rivers flowed. With scant little water left in their only flask to renew their strength, they persevered, for what choice had they? It was on the fourth day, just as they reached the crest of a hill, that the horse died, leaving them both on foot with their heavy burdens yet to carry. Before them lay a higher hill to cross and still there was no sign of a forest or mountains.

In the cool of the evening, when he spread the blanket on the ground, Bearnard gave his wife the last sip of water from his flask, and held her close, for he feared she and the baby she carried would not live another day. When morning came, he was relieved to find she had survived. He searched the brightening sky in hopes of seeing clouds, and then did his best to hide his disappointment when there were none. All they had left was hope – hope of finding water, hope of not becoming victim to desperate and ferocious animals, and hope that the child would be born alive.

Once more they set out.

It was on the fifth day, just as they reached the top of yet another hill, that a glistening beyond the trees in the glen below appeared to be a reflection of bright sunlight on water. He thought it an illusion at first, but Edana did not hesitated. Half running and half sliding, she started down the hill toward what remained of a greatly diminished, yet life-saving "L" shaped loch. It seemed her strength was somehow renewed as she threaded her way between the trees and as she crossed the glen and reached the shore, she began throwing off her heavy burdens, then her extra clothing, and at last, her tunic and skirt, all of which had become unbearably hot and heavy. In only her linen underclothing, she struggled to cross the loch's receded rocky bottom, and then waded into the glory of the cool, refreshing wetness.

Behind her, and not far behind her at that, Bearnard hesitated not as he also peeled off his heavy cloak and then each item of clothing in turn, one layer at a time as well. As eagerly as she, once in the water, he cupped his hands, drew in the cool liquid, and when he thought he could hold no more, immersed his entire naked body in the water. When he came up for air, Edana was laughing.

No more joyful sound had he ever heard, nor would he ever hear again.

At the time, he cared not, nor did he notice that there were eyes watching him from behind the bushes – eyes filled with horror and mouths that whispered, "Dealanach!" They were the eyes of those of little understanding who would give a false meaning to what they saw; a meaning that would haunt Bearnard and his descendants for years to come.

That night, they dug in the ground for pig nuts to eat, made a bed on soft leaves beneath the boughs of a tree in the forest, and slept better than they had in days. Morning brought another hot day, but the glen and the mountains reminded him of home, so Bernard imagined it to be a peaceful place in which to begin anew.

Not but three days hence, light and then dark clouds finally appeared on the horizon, a stiff wind filled the air first with the smell of dust, and at last, rain returned to Scotland. As if by some miracle, the long brown grass renewed its greenery, trickles of water in the creeks that fed the loch became rushing torrents, and dangerous animals came no more out of the mountains in search of water.

And so began a new MacGreagor village, small though it was at first. With winter coming and on at the edge of the glen between the forest and the loch, Bearnard built the barest of four walls, a thatched roof, and an outside pit for cooking. The land was good, the forest supplied more than enough firewood, and they were privy to seeing the occasional comings and goings of all manner of animals including red deer, rabbits, ducks, swans, eagles, and finally fish once more thrived in the loch.

It was clear they were not completely alone. In the distance, they could see whispers of smoke rising from the hearths of other villages, some on their side of the loch and some on the other side. As well, Bearnard often felt he was being watched. Even so, for the length of four weeks, not one visitor came to see what they were about. It was not until Bearnard walked around the bend in the lock to see about his nearest neighbor, that he understood why.

He soon encountered a pile of rocks that formed a wall of sorts between their two lands, and on the other side of the wall were three armed men with their bows at the ready and their arrows pointed directly at him. "I mean you no harm," he tried.

"You are cursed," said one.

Bearnard wrinkled his brow. "Cursed? Why say you I am cursed?"

"You bear the mark of the dealanach!"

Puzzled for a moment, Bearnard remembered walking into the water naked, and realized that by so doing, he revealed a large, bright red birthmark on his chest – a mark in the shape of a bolt of lightning. "Aye, 'twas born with the mark, but 'tis not a curse. We came from the drought in the north in search of water. If 'twas truly a curse, we'd not have lived." His explanation seemed to satisfy them, although the men invited him not to stay and visit. Nonetheless, he asked a question that had been haunting him. "Have you heard? How many in Scotland yet live?"

He waited and waited, searching the eyes of each man in turn, but when no answer came, and being of no mood to insist, Bearnard turned around and started home. He'd not gone but a few steps when one of the men behind him yelled, "Half be dead, we hear!"

With his back still to them, Bearnard stopped and hung his head. "I thank you for tellin' it." With that, he went home to share the sad news with Edana.

From that day on, he suffered but a distant relationship with his nearest neighbors, the Lennox, until he found a lost Lennox child on his side of the wall and took her home. Even then, the comment of the Lennox laird, the only man willing to speak to him, consisted of none but a brief statement of appreciation. When Edana's time came, Bernard sought a mid-wife from the Lennox, and was relieved when an elder woman agreed to help. His wife's labor was long and hard, and he was in great fear that the lack of water for so many days had injured the unborn child, but his first son was born healthy. The midwife saw that the child bore no same mark as his father, and happily announced that the curse had been lifted.

Bearnard simply smiled.

At the behest of several insistent Irish monks, a formal religion had spread across the length and breadth of Scotland. Bearnard knew little about the particulars of the religion, for the monks had not yet discovered the MacGreagor's original home in the mountains, but he found comfort in the idea that there was a higher power than he. In spring, he cleared a parcel of land, planted the few seeds he brought with him, and prayed without ceasing that the seeds would produce enough vegetables to allow the gathering of new seeds for the coming year – and perhaps make a fine winter meal or two. He prayed for nearly everything they needed, and his prayers were answered, although not often precisely as he requested.

He prayed for a horse and found a wandering mule. He received two dogs he did not pray for, and instead of bartering with the Lennox for a cow from which to get milk, butter and cheese, he ended up with a bull and a he-goat, neither of which had milk to give. Fortunately, in the opposite direction from the Lennox, albeit farther away, lived Clan Allaway. With the Allaway, he managed to trade the bull for a cow and two lambs.

It was a beginning.

What he longed for most, other than that which they needed to survive, was word of what was happening in the rest of Scotland. He thought often of those he said goodbye to and wondered if his family were the last MacGreagors alive on the earth. With no friends to speak of and no nearby road upon which strangers traveled, news came only on those rare encounters when the Lennox cared to give it, and never did they mention another MacGreagor clan.

Bearnard came across the solution to his lack of friends willing to share the news quite by accident. When the next winter approached, he being the son and grandson of MacGreagor builders, he began to construct a better home for his wife and child. This time, the eyes that often watched him from behind the trees and bushes were fascinated. At first, only one Lennox came to take a closer look, even though he offered not to help. Later, came others and these, wanting to learn the trade firsthand, helped in such a way as to lesson Bearnard's labors considerably. Soon, word spread and men came from Clans MacKellar and Battie to watch. Bearnard knew them not, but welcomed them just the same, and because they had a thirst for knowledge, he built a second cottage to house his son and the wife he would have someday. As well, wives came to see Edana and brought fresh vegetables, which greatly enhanced the MacGreagor's supper. Therefore, a friendship was finally forged amongst clans MacKellar, Battie, Lennox, and MacGreagor – although it remained a cautious one with the Lennox.

As the years passed, Bearnard sparingly bartered the three small diamonds to enhance their lives, while Edana gave him ten children, eight of which were healthy and survived. The three girls and five boys looked more like their mother than their father, with various shades of red hair, and Edana's same sparkle in their eyes. Of an evening, when he was in the mood, he recounted stories of their Viking heritage, how they once lived in a hidden castle, and how there had once been born to the MacGreagors, a giant.

Not one of his children bore a birthmark on their bodies. Even so, the rumor of the curse lived among the Lennox, to be passed down from generation to generation. When it came time for Bearnard's sons to take wives, the Lennox wanted no part of an intermarriage, and went so far as to forbid the young MacGreagor men from crossing the stonewall. As well, their young women who had often come to flirt in the MacGreagor village, where told the same.

Therefore, the three eldest sons set out to find wives among the other clans. For days they did not return, and just when Bearnard feared the death of all three, they came back with not just one wife each, but three more women and two men.

Bearnard was not pleased. The problem was in their manner of dress and he wanted no part of them. He stood in front of his cottage with his arms folded and his disbelieving eyes sternly set upon his sons. "They be English!"

"They be not English but Scots," the eldest son assured his father.

"Nary have I seen a Scot dressed in such a manner as to be wholly unworthy of settin' foot in Scotland."

"They be enslaved by the English and their dress forced upon them, but we..." the oldest son quickly glanced at his younger brothers. "We relieved the English from their burden."

"You stole them?"

"Nay," the oldest started.

"Aye," said the other two brothers in unison.

Bearnard's scowl slowly turned to a smile. "Then I am well pleased. Do the English follow you?"

"Nay," said the youngest. "'Twas what took so long. The English are good hunters, and we were often forced to hide." He walked forward and put a hand on his father's shoulder. "You have taught us well, Father, for we've not seen them in three days."

Thus, the MacGreagors became not twelve, but as the years progressed, twenty, thirty, and more. For the rest of his days, Bearnard expected to see the English come for their slaves, but he never did. He lived to be three and thirty before he passed, leaving all he carried from the north to his eldest son, including the MacGreagor stories. Now that the Vikings were long gone, there was no need to hide their heritage, and although the tip was broken off, the sword that had been handed down through the generations was also passed to his son. By then, the tip of the sword was chipped, and the long, wide blade was still in need of a good sharpening. That was the one thing Bearnard never got around to doing.

Not once, in all his years, did he hear that another MacGreagor clan had survived.

As was the way of the world, the elderly died, a crying newborn signaled a new generation, and the land and all it produced passed into the hands of the next Laird, and then the next, and continued on until a man by the name of Ronson became leader of the MacGreagors.

CHAPTER 2

IN THE ALLAWAY VILLAGE, the smell of spring was definitely in the air.

The blades of tall green grass waved in the breeze, the sky was clear, heather bloomed on the hillsides, and but a touch of snow still remained on the tops of the high mountains. Birds chirped, the sheep grazed, and there was just one thing in the world fifteen-year-old Jinny Allaway wished for more than time alone. It was a handsome husband who would suddenly appear, profess his love for her, and carry her off to a new and exciting life. Of course, spring was a time for planting and unless a man set out to find a wife early, he was not likely to do so until summer, and perhaps even autumn.

Jinny worked hard to finish her daily chores by late afternoon, so she could take a long walk and contemplate her future. Her home was not near the loch, nor even on a road well-traveled by neighbors and strangers alike. Instead, it was situated in a wide glen against a backdrop of jagged rocks and high cliffs. While Jinny found her surroundings boring and exasperating on most days, the Allaway preferred being hidden away where passing armies and feuding clans could not easily happen upon them. However, hidden away did not bode well when it came to a young woman in want of a husband.

The Allaway herd was of a good size and were often moved from clearing to clearing so the sheep could feast on the most recent growth of foliage. She walked to the end of the village glen, up a path, passed one clearing, then another and smiled when she finally laid eyes on the herd. Only two lambs had been born so far, but it was early spring and the size of the ewes' bellies gave her hope for several more. She shooed away the sheep dogs that came to greet her, nodded to the sheep herder, and continued on up the path.

As was the case for all young Allaway women, she wore the usual handed down tattered and mended brown tunic, over a yellowing shirt with long sleeves that were wide at the wrist. Her long golden hair was braided and hung down her back, with loose strands that seemed always to be in her face where they ought not to be. It was bothersome having to shove them back often, but there was little she could do about it, having neglected to put her headband on that morning, and not willing to return home to get it

At last she came to her favorite clearing, the one in which a pile of stones had been set aside by one ancestor or another, and larger flat rocks offered her a place to sit. As she made her way to the rocks she drew in the fresh air and enjoyed the many yellow and blue wild flowers from which bees were busily collecting pollen.

Abruptly, she stopped.

A small, winding stream flowed down the middle of the clearing toward the loch, and when she looked, a red deer and her newborn had ventured out into the open and were headed to the stream. The deer seemed unconcerned by Jinny's presence, although it did stare at her for a time. Eventually, the doe took a long drink, and then went back into the trees with the still stumbling fawn closely following.

Jinny smiled. She glanced at the clear blue sky, took another deep breath, and turned all the way around as though thoroughly relishing her much coveted serenity. Hers was a life of hard work with an untold number of demands put upon her daily, demands she hoped a husband and a life in a village other than the one she currently resided in, would relieve her of.

It was of her mysterious future love she was dreaming when she started across the pile of rocks. Suddenly, her foot got caught between two fairly large stones, causing her to nearly fall forward. Just in time, she put both of her hands out and caught herself. Carefully, she eased herself upright again and tried to free her foot. It would not come out, so she leaned down, and then tried to move the stones apart. Both refused to budge. Moreover, her foot was wedged at such an angle as to keep her from sitting. It hurt, but that was the least of her problems. She doubted, and with good reason, that anyone would go looking for her. Moreover, the sun was going down, and darkness meant danger.

"Help," she called out. Just as she expected, no one answered, not even the shepherd tending his flock in a clearing not far away. Again she yelled, and this time, even louder. Next, she screamed. still, she received no sign that anyone heard her, and she feared not one single soul would ever come. Again she tried to free herself, even untying her high-top shoe, but it was no use. It would surely take three stout men to move the rocks apart and even then, she knew not if she could walk or would ever walk again.

The pain had become excruciating, and she was about to give in to a feeling of desperation when the situation got far worst. Behind her, she heard the unmistakable hiss of a wildcat. Slowly and ever so carefully, she pulled her knife out of its sheath and turned to look. To her horror, it was the largest cat she had ever seen and it was poised to jump on her back.

BEARNARD HAD LONG SINCE passed, as had more than seven generations by the time Kam MacGreagor, the first born son of Laird Ronson MacGreagor, was born. At twenty, his was a normal life, although uninteresting by his standards. Uninteresting that is, except when he and his friends, William and Durell went on the hunt for red deer in the high mountains. On this occasion, deer had been scarce and so far, all they managed to shoot were three rather large hares, the carcasses of which hung from William's belt. It was getting late, and all three agreed to head home to enjoy a good meal, and climb into bed.

On a well-traveled, tree lined road that lie on the same side of the loch as the MacGreagor village, the three young men chatted about the usual things – food, hunting and women, although not in that precise order. William and Durell were older, married, and happily so, or so they claimed.

Kam was yet unmarried, but he hoped to remedy that soon. He suddenly raised his hand to stop the others and pulled his horse to an abrupt halt.

"What is it?" William whispered, stopping his horse as well. Rumors of clan wars, and even a war between the English and the Scots seemed unending lately, and it was always prudent to keep an eye out for danger. Durell, William noticed, had turned his horse enough so he could keep watch behind them.

"Silence," Kam muttered.

William sat up a little straighter on his horse and tried to discern precisely what danger may lay ahead. It took a moment, but at length, he heard a woman cry for help. "'Tis a trap," he muttered.

Kam nodded. "As well it may be, but if 'tis not, what then?"

Durell agreed. "Aye, she sounds in great need. Are we to leave a fair lass to die?"

William chuckled, "Fair? More likely 'tis a lass long past her bonnie days, with a husband and ten..."

"Shhhh," Kam insisted. The cry was faint, but he clearly heard it for a third time. The only question was – from which direction did it come. When he glanced at his friends, William was pointing east and Durell was pointing west. Kam rolled his eyes. To his way of thinking William was right, so he turned his horse into the forest, headed east, and began to thread his way between the trees and the bushes. Again he heard her cry out, and this time it was louder and sounded more urgent, so he quickened the pace of his horse. A short time later, he reached the edge of a clearing.

There she was, a young woman of perhaps fourteen who appeared to be somehow unable to move. Worse still, on the other side of her, a wildcat was preparing to attack.

WHEN THE UNUSUALLY large wildcat began to leap into the air Jinny let out a terrifying scream. At that exact moment an arrow pierced the cat's heart. The cat cried out, fell to the ground, and moved not again. Stunned, Jinny slowly turned to look in the direction from which the arrow came. Farther away than most men could shoot and still hit their mark, the tall, handsome Kam MacGreagor reloaded his bow just in case, and then urged his horse toward her.

Her heart skipped a beat when she saw how handsome he was, and she almost wished he would stay away, for she found the whole situation embarrassing. When she dreamed of meeting such a man as he, she was perfectly presentable, with a band holding the loose strands of hair off her face, and standing as tall as her frame would allow. Just now, her hair was in her eyes, she could not move, let alone stand tall, and the clothing she wore was as old as she was. Even so, she could not take her eyes off him as he urged his horse closer, and then swung down. Two more men on horseback came out of the forest as well, but they stayed back, and Jinny paid them no attention at all.

First, the stranger made certain the cat was truly dead, slipped an unspent arrow back in his sheath, and then set his bow on the ground. At last, his eyes met hers and she was so enamored, she could hardly take a breath. "My foot is caught," she finally managed to say as she shoved her hair back.

"So I see." He studied the situation for a moment, and then nodded toward the weapon she held in her hand. "You'll not need that."

"Oh," she shyly muttered as she put her knife away.

"I must first move the stone."

When he leaned down in front of her, she was tempted to steady herself by holding on to him, but she reconsidered and prepared herself to fall instead. To her, it was a mammoth feat, but to him the weight of the large rock seemed no challenge at all. Before she could mutter another word, he tossed the rock aside, and then instantly grabbed her arm to make certain she would not fall.

"I feared no one would come," she confessed. "I thank you."

He paid little attention. Instead, he helped her sit on one of the large rocks, took hold of her lower leg, gently pulled her shoe off, and surveyed the damage. "It swells," he muttered. "Can you move it?"

She slowly turned her foot to one side and then the other. It was painful and made her bite her lower lip to keep from moaning, but it did not seem broken. Next, she wiggled her toes and then tried to reassure him with a smile. "There, you see I am fine." She glanced at the other two, and then turned her attention back to the handsome one. "I've not seen you afore."

"Nor I you. I am Kam. We are from Clan MacGreagor."

She did her best to hide her shock. "Oh."

Kam ignored the familiar look on her face. "And you are?"

"I am Jinny from Clan Allaway."

"Well, Jinny from Clan Allaway, you cannae walk. Therefore, I shall take you home."

"Nay, you mustn't..." she was too late for in the space of a heartbeat, he handed her shoe to her, swooped her up, and had her in his strong arms. He stepped over the rocks, took her to his horse, lifted her up, and did not let go until she was had a firm grip of the horse's mane.

He reached for the reins, and then asked, "Why do you say I mustn't take you home?"

This time when her heart skipped a beat it was out of distress. "Forgive me, I only meant..."

"'Tis because we MacGreagors are cursed?"

"Nay," she said as sincerely as she could manage.

Kam motioned for the others to come forward. "We are not cursed, Jinny, 'tis a falsehood."

"But the Lennox say of the tree..."

"Aye, that much be true. I was but a wee laddie when lightning struck the tree. It glowed red for three full days and when it was done, the black mark held the shape of the lightnin.'"

"It stands this day still near the wall between our land and that of the Lennox," William offered when he drew near, He too dismounted, checked to make certain the cat was dead, and then picked it up, and put the carcass over the back of his horse. Next, he went back and picked Kam's bow up off the ground.

Jinny wrinkled her brow, "But 'tis true the tree dinna burn?"

"That be true right enough," Durell admitted. "Or so I have heard."

"Oh, I see, but..."

"Jinny of Clan Allaway?" Kam interrupted.

"What?"

"I cannae take you home lest you tell me which is the shortest way."

Hers was a nervous giggle when she pointed to the path at the other end of the clearing. "'Tis not far."

He turned his back to her, pulled on the horse's reins, and led the way on foot down the path. Jinny's mind raced with excitement. He had come finally, the man who would claim to love her, marry her, and take her to a life of constant peace and joy. Though he did not often look at her, his eyes were the perfect shade of blue, his hair more red than brown, and his beard neatly trimmed. Moreover, he had bathed recently and smelled of...of chopped wood, her favorite aroma. She was so charmed by him, she hardly felt any pain at all, even as her body swayed with the movement of the horse.

If only he were not a MacGreagor.

It was said in the village of the Allaway, that it was not of good health to bathe often, although it was rumored the MacGreagors paid no attention to their health. From the looks of Kam, Jinny could see nothing at all amiss with his well-being. In fact, a healthier lad she had never seen. There were other rumors about the MacGreagors too, and now it seemed she might pause somewhat before she believed them. When she glanced back, the other two looked just as healthy.

"You be light as a feather," Kam said finally. "Dinna they feed you well?"

"Aye," was all she said in return. Secretly, she wished he would slow down so she could stay with him longer, if only for a brief time more. Unfortunately, his was a hurried walk as though he thought it more urgent to get her home than she believed it was. Too soon, they came in full view of the village.

Not unlike all the other villages, the Allaway's had one distinct advantage – they built their cottages not far from a rather wide creek, allowing easy access to plenty of water. Several wooden carts sat in a row near the largest of the cottages, and the paths were lined with what appeared to be carefully positioned herb plants, making the herbs with which to please their palates easily gathered. The people on the paths stopped to stare as soon as they spotted the strangers, and several Allaways were standing around a fire. Moreover, the alarm on the faces of the people seemed to markedly increase when they realized Jinny was with the strangers.

"I know them," said one of the Allaway men. "They be MacGreagors." The Allaway did not abruptly arm themselves, for they thought not of the MacGreagors as a threat, at least not the kind of threat to begin a battle.

"Aye," said another, pointing at Kam. "And he be Laird MacGreagor's eldest son."

A laird's son and the next to lead his clan was not what Jinny wished Kam to be. As the daughter of a laird, her dream was of a far more pleasant life, one in which the father was not always in need of sharing his time. Before Kam could halt the horse and reach up for her, she looked to see where her sister was. Just as she feared, Owena was with the others where the light of the fire made her look even more beautiful than usual. There was not a man alive, not that Jinny had ever seen, that did not prefer Owena to her, and she hoped she might have more time to impress Kam before she was forced to step aside. Oh well, there was nothing she could do about that.

"She is hurt," Kam said. He halted the horse, reached for her, and pulled Jinny down. He let her stand on one foot for a second, and then once more swooped her up into his strong arms. It was then he noticed Owena and briefly paused, although he did not stare at her, but instead, walked right past her. Jinny found that somewhat encouraging.

One of the men rushed to open the door to the laird's house, and motioned for Kam to take Jinny inside. So tall was Kam that he had to lean down to enter, which astounded the other men and made them mutter. From inside, Jinny's mother cried out at the sight of her daughter, and then covered her mouth. Four much younger children seemed to cower in the corner, afraid of the stranger.

The inside of the laird's cottage was larger than it appeared to be from the outside. A variety of weapons hung at the ready on the walls, and although there were several windows, they were too small to let in much light. Instead, a warm glow came from an impressively large stone hearth at one end of the room, where the cooking and the eating normally took place. Curtains made of woven heather hung in two side doorways both of which led to sleeping rooms, and the entire cottage held the familiar smell of mutton stew.

"'Tis just an ankle," Jinny assured her mother.

The clan's mistress motioned for Kam to set her daughter in a chair near the table, and as soon as he did, she knelt in front of her child, raised the hem of Jinny's skirt, and had a look for herself. By then, it was not only swollen, it was starting to bruise. "You must put your foot in the cold water of the creek."

"But mother..." Jinny protested.

"She is right," her father said, himself hurrying through the front door.

Jinny objected. "But father, the water still bears the cold of winter" She noticed when Kam moved away, and also noticed his reaction when her sister came in. All too often she had seen that look in a man's eyes before, and knew exactly what it meant. She turned her gaze instead on the father she adored, and appreciated his sympathetic expression. However, instead of picking his daughter up and taking her to the creek, Laird Allaway turned to size up the MacGreagor.

"He killed a wildcat that was..." Jinny started to say.

"On our land or his?" her father interrupted.

"I..." a frustrated Jinny tried to answered. "He shot the cat just as it was..."

"Well, MacGreagor, is the cat on your land or mine?"

"Yours," Kam answered.

"Good, we are in great need of the hide."

"Father, perhaps you should let the MacGreagor have it, for..." Jinny again tried.

Laird Allaway gasped. "Let the MacGreagor have it? Have you gone daft?"

Jinny bowed her head, "I only thought that since he saved me, you might..."

Laird Allaway disagreed. "Savin' you is all well and good, but the cat was shot on our land and the hide needs be ours too."

Jinny drew in a frustrated breath. Her father was well known for his stubbornness, and arguing with him was usually a waste of time. Worse than that, Kam had still not taken his eyes off of Owena. Once more, Jinny tried not to let it bother her, but it did – this time it truly did bother her.

"I best be gone," Kam said finally. "'Tis late and we hope to be home before dark."

"Aye, best you..." Laird Allaway paused before he finished his sentence. "Have you a wife?" When Kam was slow to answer, Laird Allaway attempted to explain. "I've two daughters in need of husbands, and..."

"Husbands? He is a MacGreagor," Mistress Allaway gasped.

"Aye, but what choice have I, wife? Shall I give them to a MacKellar or a Battie? Are they not always at war? Therefore, how long before we have dead daughters? And the Lennox have no lads this spring that have reached marrying age. Besides, was it not you who said you wish to keep your daughters close to you forever?"

Mistress Allaway tried to argue, but he held up his hand to stop her. "The MacGreagors are but a pleasant ride away." He had spoken, and even the chagrinned look on his wife's face was not going to change his mind. At length, he turned his attention back to Kam. "Well, what say you? Which of my daughters shall you have?" He pointed first at Jinny and then at Owena.

Kam looked from Owena to Jinny and back again. "I have not yet my father's permission to marry."

"Your father must give his permission?" a surprised Laird Allaway asked. "Never have I heard of such a thing."

Kam smiled, "You have not heard of my father's peculiar ways?"

Laird Allaway frowned and then slowly began to smile, "Perhaps I have at that. Then you shall come back when your father gives his permission." It was a command and not a request, to which Kam nodded.

Owena went to stand behind Jinny's chair and slowly lifted her eyes to Kam's. "Dinna choose me, for I canna bear to live apart from my sister. I shall not marry until Jinny is wed to a MacGreagor as well."

"I see," was all Kam had to say.

"Perhaps you have a brother?" Owena persisted.

"A brother of marryin' age?" Kam muttered. "Aye, but..."

Laird Allaway looked unusually pleased. "Very well. Bring your brother around and let me have a look at him, but first, bring me the wildcat so my lads can skin it."

That should have been the end of it, for Jinny already knew which sister Kam would wish to marry. All hope was lost forever and her despair allowed the pain of her injury to make itself abundantly known. Yet something quite unexpected happened – something that gave her hope. Kam came to her and began to lift her back into his arms. "I shall take you to the creek." He gently picked lifted her and carried her out the door. Jinny could not help herself, she wrapped both her arms around his neck and laid her head on his shoulder. It might be, after all, her only chance to make a precious memory, one of a found and then lost love, that she could keep near and dear to her heart.

Every eye was on them, when he took her to a rock at the edge of the creek and then carefully set her down. Even then, Kam did not leave, nor did he look to see where Owena was. Instead, he put his hands on his hips and stared at Jinny. "Well, are you to put your foot in the water, or am I to do it for you?"

Jinny answered, "I shall do it, but I must admit I so dread the cold."

"I blame you not, but it must be done."

Slowly and deliberately, she eased her hurt foot into the freezing water, all the while trying not to let a tear roll down her cheek. When she looked, Kam seemed pleased with her, and then he walked away. She watched him go to William's horse, retrieve the wildcat's carcass, and give it to an Allaway standing near the fire. Soon, he mounted, nodded to William and Durell, and then rode away without looking back – not even at Owena.

Perhaps Jinny's love had come after all. There were lads in the world who preferred good wives, not just bonnie ones. There had to be! Then again, the proof remained to be seen. He might not come back, not for either of them, and that she could abide far better than if he claimed

Owena instead. Still, she had hope, and hope was all she had until he came back – if he came back.

CHAPTER 3

ON THE CREST OF THE same hill Bearnard and Edana climbed when they first discovered the loch, Ronson MacGreagor stood with his legs apart and his arms folded, watching yet another wrestling match between his two eldest sons, Kam and Glendon. Already they were at it, tossing each other this way and that, and it had been but a short time since the MacGreagors climbed out of bed. It was spring, they had chores to do, and no time to waste on petty arguments.

Soon, the cows would begin their morning complaint of having not yet been milked, and the shepherds would head out to see how well the dogs tended the herd in the night. That, plus his sons shouting and wrestling was keeping Ronson from hearing the pleasing whisper of the wind as it swept through the glen. His sons were far too competitive. They seemed always to be racing to do this or that, trying to prove which was the strongest or had the best wits. Ronson found it most exasperating, and his frown said as much, even though neither of his sons bothered to notice him.

Each morning without fail, Ronson climbed the hill just to feel the breeze on his face and savor the peace and comfort it bestowed upon him. Be it a gentle or a strong wind mattered not, it was always the perfect way to begin a day that promised hard work and little reward.

From his vantage point, Ronson could see part of the shortest and all of the longest length of the "L" shaped loch. As well, he could see a glistening, winding river that originated high in the snowcapped mountains. Smoke rose from villages on the other side of the loch, the inhabitants of which rarely traveled around the water, save to hunt or make their way to the King's castle in Edinburgh. The peaceful and often misty glen the MacGreagors called home, offered good land upon which sheep and cattle grazed, an abundance of trees, hills, and a close neighbor on but one side. The makeshift wall that still only consisted of piles of stones, yet marked where the MacGreagor land ended and the Lennox land began. Its main purpose was to keep the livestock separated, and on most occasions, it served its purpose well. The Lennox village had grown considerably too since the days of old, although it still lay far enough around the natural bend in the loch, so as not to be easily seen.

On the same side of the water, albeit in the opposite direction of the Lennox village, lived Clan Allaway. Their other neighbors, Clan MacKellar and Clan Battie lived much farther away and lately had become involved in a blood feud, which the MacGreagors, the Allaway and the Lennox happily stayed out of. Over the years, an animal path on the other side of the hills to the north of them had become a road well-traveled, and stretched all the way from the east coast of Scotland to the west coast. The road brought occasional visitors, those unaware of the MacGreagor curse, and much sought after news.

Normally of a morning, Ronson's wife came to stand beside him on the hill, just to spend a few private moments with her husband. They were the parents of nine, four of which survived the last fever, and another one was on the way. Therefore, privacy was precious, always in great demand, and rarely satisfied long enough before the labors of the day were once more forced upon them.

Even without looking he knew she was there. Instead he continued to watch his wayward sons, hoping neither would suffer a wound or a broken bone. It mattered not about what his sons argued, for at twenty and nineteen years, they were constantly at odds over the least little thing. "They need wives," he muttered.

"Aye," said Mayzie. When she put an arm around him, he responded by putting both of his arms around her. Their clothing had seen better days, and they wore enough layers to keep them warm until the work demanded they take off a layer or two. Both dressed in brown tunics, his short over baggy, rope-tied pants, and hers long and belted. They had on waist-high leggings, vests and were fortunate enough to have long cloaks made of fleece, which neither needed in the warmth of this particular spring morning.

Nothing gave him more pleasure than having Mayzie in his arms, if even for a brief moment. It was she who made his life bearable. When the gentle breeze he loved so well lifted strands of light brown hair off the fair skin of her face, he smiled. As well, he found peace in her warm brown eyes, just as he had the first time he saw her. That day was like any other, made divinely special when a monk, escorting several young women to the abbey, stopped to rest near the village. Ronson knew the instant her eyes met his, that Mayzie was the wife he'd longed for. When he asked for her, the other young women giggled, but she did not. To his amazement, Mayzie climbed out of the cart and took up a position right beside him. Bribing the monk to let him marry her without delay cost Ronson one lamb and two border collie pups, but having her was worth that and more. Even after all their years together, he savored her willing touch, and inevitably drew her closer. "A wife shall quiet them and perhaps even make the lads more sensible."

She softly giggled. "Perhaps, and perhaps not."

"Laugh if you will, but look what you have done for me. Am I not well mannered, settled, and attentive, just as you said I was to be?"

"Almost."

He leaned back to look into her eyes. "Lass, of what do you speak?"

"Do you not have two daughters? Yet when they are quarrelsome, you are not so very attentive to them."

She was right, and he well knew it, so he pulled her back into his arms. "Mayzie, I understand not the cause of my daughters' unhappiness. Their world is not the same as the lads."

"Nay, they are not the same, nor should they be. The duties given to all lasses are different, their loves and hates are different, and without lasses in the world, who would marry your unruly sons?"

He narrowed his eyes. "*My* unruly sons, is it? From the time they were but wee bairns, was it not you who taught them good from bad?"

She rolled her eyes. "You expected *me* to teach them good from bad? 'Tis a bit late to be tellin' me that!"

Ronson could not help but grin. "Again I have blundered."

She laid her head back against his chest. "Take it not to heart, for you have taught them a thing of far more value."

"Which is?"

"How very well a husband is to love his wife."

Ronson took a joyful breath, laid the side of his face against the top of her head, and closed his eyes. "I thank God each day for sendin' me such a good lass to love."

She enjoyed his embrace for a moment more, pulled away, and started down the hill, "I best go tend my chores before you tell God you have changed your mind."

Still grinning, he folded his arms again and watched her scurry down the hill to the village of his birth. Ronson was getting on in years and already he could feel his strength dwindling. Such were the ways of men, for they lived but short lives, if they lived long at all.

THE VILLAGE HAD GROWN considerably since that poorly put together cottage protected Bearnard and Edana from their first winter. Bearnard's building skills had been handed down through the generations, enabling well-constructed cottages of stones drudged from the banks of the loch, and held together with thick mortar made of heather and sand. They were careful not to build too close to the loch for fear of a flood, or too close to the trees in case of fire. A good portion of the forest had been cleared on the flat land. The paths between the cottages, and those leading in several directions away from the village, were well worn, and whispers of smoke bore proof of growing villages on the other side of the water. Even so, the colorful land where an array of different shades of heather and bluebells grew on hillsides, provided plenty of room for a comfortable life. It included a large vegetable garden, and was dotted with grazing horses, sheep, and five milk cows.

Theirs was a very fine village, and all the MacGreagors professed to be happy there.

The only blemish on the MacGreagor land, in Ronson's opinion, was that old dead and scarred tree that had been hit by a lightning strike some years before. Not only did it leave a mark in the same image as lightning, it was wrapped all the way around the trunk. Naturally, the tree had long since died and no longer bore leaves. Therefore, it did look a little ominous in the light of a full moon. Even he had to admit as much. Ronson aimed to hitch the horses up to stout ropes and pull it out of the ground someday, but he never seemed to get around to it.

People sometimes came to the Lennox side of the wall just to get a good look at the lightning tree, which annoyed the MacGreagors. Still, even with the tree gone, people likely would not forget the curse. There were other rumors about them too, none of which were true or bothered the MacGreagors. They were pleased to mind their own business, take from the land only what they needed, and to leave the rest of the world to its own pleasures.

After the merriment of their yearly harvest feast, the time came for the patching of the old and the building of new cottages. More often than not, a room was added to an older cottage, allowing families with the most children to spread out a little more. As well, new cottages were constantly in need for such a time as a young man wanted to make a home for his bride – if he could find one that would agree to marry into a cursed clan.

After the latest sickness took the lives of the weak among them, the MacGreagors numbered less than a hundred and twenty souls, thirty of which were below the age of ten. They had dogs that were trained to help the sheep herders, enough horses to haul the heavy loads, and for the men to ride. Chickens roamed freely on the paths between the cottages, a flock of ducks normally held close to the shore of the loch, and if there was any curse upon them at all, it was due to a mule they named Calla.

No one knew from where Calla had come, and no other clan sought to claim it; or indeed was willing to admit any knowledge of it. Why, was not a secret to anyone, especially Ronson. Calla was not inclined to work no matter the coaxing. In fact, more often than not, she was spotted sitting on her haunches munching on the tall grass at the edge of the forest, that is, when the mule was not eyeing the well-tended vegetable garden. It was therefore the chore of the children to see that Calla was kept well away and it was often a full time chore. The children had one very helpful advocate, however. When Calla began to bray her resistance to the children, a Tawny Owl often flew out of the forest, and as if annoyed by the sound, dove down in an attempt to clip one of Calla's ears. The mere sight of the owl made Calla turn right around, and trot away in an attempt to find some measure of cover.

Such always made the children laugh and the adults smile.

For the most part, the lives of the MacGreagors centered on hunting and growing enough to eat, staying warm in winter, and staying out of clan disputes of which there were many. Fortunately, they were far enough away from the King's castle in Edinburgh to avoid being drawn into battles with England. Nevertheless, there seemed always to be warnings of pending wars to come. Sometimes, while standing atop or on the hillsides, they saw dust clouds in the distance, that evidenced great movements of men and horses traveling in one direction or another. It was just a matter of time until they too were drawn in – or so everyone feared.

Presently, Ronson was far more concerned with seeing that his sons married strong, healthy wives who could give them strong, healthy sons. That the women be of good sense, kind, and not so very troublesome was every father's desire. Ronson lifted the bullhorn he wore on a string around his neck and gave it one short, soft blast. Immediately, his sons stopped wrestling, stood up and looked his direction. So also did the rest of the clan, but Ronson ignored them. Instead, he motioned for his sons to come, which eased the minds of the others, who soon returned to what they were about. In no time at all, Kam, the eldest, and Glendon, a little more than a year younger, started up the hill. Both had dirt smudged faces and auburn hair that could use a good scrubbing. Kam looked remarkably like his father, and Glendon resembled his mother with her same brown eyes.

"Lads, why do you not finish your cottages? 'Tis spring, the lasses become eager to marry in spring, and you've nothin' to offer."

"Father, I care not to take a wife until next year," Glendon said. "I am but nineteen, and I see not a reason to rush."

Ronson wrinkled his brow in disapproval. "And you, Kam, have you no interest in takin' a wife?"

Kam smirked as he brushed a leaf off his shirt sleeve. "I shall have the most fetchin' wife in all of Scotland."

"You," Glendon shot back. "Who would marry you?"

Kam tightened the muscles in his forearms and doubled his fists. "I've a better chance than you, for I am tenfold the more handsome."

Glendon returned his brother's glare. "You imagine it, do you? Father, I have changed my mind. I shall marry, and a far bonnier lass than Kam."

Kam leered, "Too late, for I have already seen the fairest in the land."

"When?" Glendon wanted to know.

"On the hunt last. She is an Allaway. We happened upon her sister who was..."

Glendon's jaw dropped. "You have seen Owena?"

Kam was just as amazed. "You know her?"

"I do, and I saw her well before you. Therefore, I claim her to be mine!" Glendon squared his shoulders and doubled his fists as well.

Kam just laughed. "You cannae claim her, she is..."

Exasperated, Ronson took a deep breath. "Lads, soon I shall give my permission, but know this; neither of you are handsome enough to entice a bonnie wife if you've no cottage to take her to. I say, let the lad with a finished cottage have first choice, be she Owena Allaway or not." He did not have to say another word, for both boys scurried down the hill to their unfinished cottages and went right to work.

"That should do it," Ronson muttered.

At last he felt the wind on his face and paused for a time to enjoy it before he began his day. "An Allaway bride." He looked up to the heavens. "Aye, they shall fight over this Owena, but 'twill not be the first time a MacGreagor fought for the lass of his choice. Even so, I pray they shall not kill each other in the process." At that uneasy thought, Ronson shook his head.

Fortunately, there was much to do before the cottages would be complete, and perhaps by then, one or both of his sons would change his mind. They had doors to hang, tables and stools to build out of wood that was already cut and measured, and then of course, there was a box bed to assemble. That winter, Mayzie spent many a cold night sewing mattresses and stuffing them with a combination of feathers and wool, to be laid on benches – providing her sons had benches to put them on.

Once more Ronson looked over the land. It was indeed the beginning of spring, evidenced by the animals that were about to bring forth a new generation of offspring. Calla was nowhere to be seen, which always marked the beginning of a good day. Girls were going off to tend the milking, Children were headed to the garden, and husbands and wives were wishing each other a good morning before the husband left, and the wife went back inside to begin another day of sewing and preparing food.

For Ronson, spring was a peaceful time, a new time, and a pleasant time in the MacGreagor glen, especially when greeted by the sweet whisper of the morning wind. In three days there was to be a celebration – a great celebration, for on that particular evening, Ronson intended to not only give his sons permission to marry, but to pass to Kam the ancient sword that would make him the next laird.

THERE WAS NO MISTAKING it, for when Laird Tremaine Lennox began to blow his horn, the one carefully made from the horn of a very large Scottish bull, there was some sort of trouble to be had.

Ronson MacGreagor was halfway down the side of the hill, cringed when he heard the sound, turned around, and headed back up. He feared one day the blasting of Laird Lennox's horn might truly alert them to a clan war, a fire, a fierce animal, or worse, an English attack. So far it had not, and he doubted there was anything to worry about on this fine morning either. He had an inkling of what might be the matter, so he carefully scanned his land again to see if he could find Calla. He could not, and that particular happenstance always caused his shoulders to slump.

Slowly, Ronson turned to look toward the stonewall that separated their two lands. Just as he suspected, Laird Lennox stood with one hand on his hip, and the other outstretched thereby pointing the tip of his bullhorn directly at Calla. "I've half a mind to do away with that mule," Ronson muttered. When he looked back, the MacGreagors were watching him, waiting to see if they should be concerned. As usual, he shook his head. They laughed or waved, and then returned to

their chores. He was laird and could, and probably should, ask one of
the other men to go get Calla, but the excuse was the same – all the men
were needed to care for the animals and the people. In the end, Ronson
was the overseer, the supervisor, the laird, and the one without whom
the clan could get along very well.

Ronson sighed. The passing of the generations had softened the
relationship between the two clans, but not enough to allow his sons to
marry the daughters of the Lennox. Although the Lennox were still a
bit standoffish on occasion, the two clans managed various friendships,
especially among the older children, of which his eldest daughter,
Bradana, was one. Even if the Lennox forbid contact with the
MacGreagors, it could not be helped, for the hunters depended on
hunters from all the clans to spread the news and warn them of danger.
A day or two without news, and a Lennox or a MacGreagor would
come to speak of something, each quite naturally remaining on their
own side of the wall.

Facing the land of the Lennox once more, Ronson halfheartedly
waved to Laird Lennox, and started down the hill to retrieve the most
stubborn and useless mule in all the world. On his way past the garden,
he stopped to pull a white carrot out of the ground and shake the soil
off. He frowned, as he always did, at the lightning tree, and then walked
to the wall.

Laird Lennox was considerably older than Ronson, although the
MacGreagors did not know by how many years exactly. It was true,
however, that Laird Lennox' hair continued to turn a lighter shade of
gray each year. As most men did, Lennox wore his long hair pulled
back and tied with string. His speckled beard, however, was mostly the
same shade of red as rusted iron, as were his eyebrows and his thick
mustache.

Lennox still had one hand on his hip when Ronson approached.
"Calla got in our garden in the night, and ate three yellow squash. Have
we not enough on our hands to keep the rabbits out of the garden?"

Ronson wrinkled his brow. "Three yellow squash and the mule yet lives?"

"MacGreagor, if I though squash would kill that mule, I'd gladly give over the whole row."

Ronson held back his smile and instead rolled his eyes. "Because you hate squash!"

Lennox turned his gaze downward, stroked his beard for a moment, and then glanced behind him just to make certain no one could hear him. "Aye, but 'tis my wife, you see. She delights in the many ways of cookin' it so she might let the skins harden and thus make dippers, and all other manner of things out them. I tell you, she even mixes squash in my pottage. 'Twill surely be my ruination." He suddenly thought better of his complaint, "You'll not tell my wife, will you?

"Well now, I am tempted. Perhaps you might claim Calla to be yours and not mine?" When Lennox stood taller and glowered, Ronson feared he had gone too far. "Better yet, perhaps we might somehow tempt Calla to take up residence on the other side of the loch."

"How? We cannae even tempt her to stay on your side of the wall."

Ronson held up the carrot and waited for Calla to spot it. Normally, a carrot was enough to get the mule to follow him home, but with a full stomach, Calla simply sat down and began to bray. Laird Lennox put both hands over his ears and shouted, "Foulest noise in the world!" As abruptly as it began, the braying stopped, causing Lennox to drop his hands and both men to look to see what the matter might be. Just in time, Calla headed into the trees to once more protect its ears from the swooping Tawny Owl.

Even Laird Lennox smiled at the sight.

Ronson took the occasion to change the subject. "I hear tell the monks have taken to leavin' their Abby in search of new worshipers."

"I hear the same." Lennox remembered the bullhorn in his hand, looped the string back around his neck, and let the horn rest on his chest. "I've no time to visit the Abby more than 'tis necessary. Come to think of it, I've not been these three years."

"I have never been."

Lennox did not seem shocked by the revelation. "If the monk comes, he shall want to collect the tithe, and 'tis our duty to allow it, at least in the good years."

"And in the bad?"

Lennox paused to think for a moment. "We've the people and the animals to feed, or there shall be nor more good years, thus deprivin' the Abby of all future tithin'."

"I agree." Indeed, his thinking sounded rational enough to Ronson. He'd only spoken to two monks in his entire life; one was when a man dressed in a long, brown robe got lost and needed directions to find the road. The other was when he married Mayzie. The monk seemed pleasant enough, but then, most people did at first meeting. "About the tithe. How is it precisely measured?"

"Well, I have heard that if a lad has ten sheep, he is to give one to the Abby."

"And if he only has nine?" Ronson asked.

Perplexed, Lennox shifted his eyes back and forth. "Then he can only tithe when he has all ten. The tithe is to feed the hungry among us, or so I have been told."

Ronson stared at the ground. "Aye, the hungry. Does the king not care for the hungry?"

That made Lennox loudly scoff. "The king? When have you ever seen the king come to see who is hungry and who is not?"

"True, I have never seen him."

"Well, MacGreagor, I've work to do. See that you take that mule with you when you go, or I shall surely shoot it."

Ronson nodded, although he was tempted to leave Calla there. If Lennox did away with Calla, surely Ronson could not be blamed. On the other hand, even though the mule caused a great deal of consternation, it also provided some measure of entertainment for the children. More than one of the boys managed to get Calla to let him ride, that is, when Calla was of a mood to. Therefore, tempted though he was, he decided to try once more to lure the mule back to his side of the wall.

Clearly, the carrot would not work, but there was another way. Occasionally, but not often, music peeked Calla's interest, so Ronson lifted his baritone voice in song, reciting the only children's verse he knew, and sure enough, Calla came out of the trees and began to follow. He was relieved, for he would not miss as much work as he feared. He glanced back in time to see the mule jump over a low portion of the wall, and made a mental note to send the men to add more rocks to that particular place. The men were always adding more rocks, and it never seemed to help, but he could think of nothing else to do. Again he looked back, saw that the mule was still following, frowned again at the lightning tree, walked past the garden, and headed for the shore of the loch.

When Ronson stopped singing, he did not notice, nor did he care that Calla had stopped. He had already wasted too much time, and now it was up to the children to keep the mule out of the MacGreagor garden.

CHAPTER 4

THE INHABITANTS OF the small Allaway village herded sheep, sold the wool in spring, made various other goods to barter, and did as well for themselves as most other clans. The women were excellent weavers, the men were strong, and the children were dutiful for the most part.

It was washing day, a day Jinny dreaded, but it was spring, young men were expected to come around some time soon, and if they were to attract a husband, they best be presentable – or so their father demanded that very morning. The Allaway women complained that washing clothes muddied the water supply near the village, so the sisters were put upon to carry the basket a good distance downstream where the water was deep enough. Stones of various sizes and shapes lined most of the creek bank, but there was a sandy place suitable for their needs.

"He means to marry us off," said a disgruntled Owena.

As soon as they reached the sandy shore, Owena let go of the handle on her side of the heavy basket, causing it to tip and thereby leaving Jinny to manage the full weight of it by herself. Just in time, Jinny set her side of the basket down, and flashed her sister an annoyed look. Owena promptly ignored it.

Instead, Owena chose a large rock to sit on at the edge of the creek. She wore her long blond hair in a braid down her back, with a woven, yet colorful band around her head to keep the loose strands off her face. Always aware of the clansmen who liked to look at her, and might appear at any moment, she fanned her full blue skirt out, flattened the wrinkles, and then drew in a refreshing breath of air.

As she usually did, Jinny dismissed her agitation and began dumping the soiled clothing on the sand, so she could refill the basket with those that were washed. It was a full load on this particular day and included items for all eight members of her family.

There was no such thing as new clothing, not in Jinny's world anyway. Her mother got the new cloth, made something of it for herself and her father, added patches when needed, and then handed what she replaced of her things down first to Owena. By the time Jinny got them, there were even more patches. However, only three patches had been added to her latest hand-me-down skirt, all three of which were more toward the back than the front. It was that skirt she hoped to be wearing when Kam MacGreagor came back to marry her – if he came back.

"Did you not hear me?" Owena asked. "Father means to marry us off."

There were days when her sister's demand on her attention irritated her more than usual, and this was one of them. "He means to marry *you* off." Although washing in the creek was hard work, Jinny did not mind that Owena was not helping. Long ago, Owena made an intentional practice of doing everything wrong just to irritate Jinny, and it was much easier and far more efficient just to do it herself.

Jinny took off her shoes and once more examined the side of her foot. Thankfully, the bluish bruise had already turned yellow and even that was fading away. As was her custom, she carefully set her shoes side by side and out of the way so they would not get wet. Next, she leaned forward, reached between her legs, and grabbed ahold of the hem of her full-length brown skirt. She pulled it forward, and then tucked the length in the front of her belt. That done, she grabbed a skirt, and waded into the water. Already the water seemed warmer than it had when Kam insisted she put her hurt foot in. She held up the skirt, looked for stains, submerged it in the water, and then began to scrub the front with a bar of soap she made herself out of mutton fat, potash, and lye.

Jinny liked staying busy while she waited for Kam to return, and while she worked, she imagined just how it would be. Naturally, he would ride the same horse, but it would be obvious the horse had been given a good washing, which would make its coat shine in the sunlight. Kam too would wear clean clothing as well and smell of – chopped wood, just as he had before. Indeed, it was only a matter of time until he would come for her. Of that, she was certain, and then she would be free of the madness that had become her mundane life.

There was only one problem: Owena.

Jinny could not be absolutely certain Kam would choose her instead of Owena, no matter how hard she tried to make herself believe he would. When the time came, she had half a mind to lock her sister in a cottage. Unfortunately, she loved Owena, no matter her many faults, and could never do such a thing. Jinny sighed, grabbed yet another skirt from atop the pile and began to wash it. She scrubbed stains that never seemed to come out with soap, rinsed the skirt, looked it over, front and back, decided it was clean enough, and tossed it in the basket.

"I shall marry Kam, for he is the son of a laird, and I shall be the mistress of his clan."

Jinny was not surprised, Owena had said as much at various times over the last few days. She dinna bother looking at her sister as she picked up the next item to be washed. "You expect to have servants, I dare suppose."

"Aye, I shall have many servants."

"Sister, you dream of bein' a queen, not a mistress. Clans dinna have servants."

"I know, but I shall call them helpers instead. Mother has helpers."

"When there is much to be done. Otherwise, she cares for us herself the same as any other lass."

Owena shrugged. "Well, I shan't be so foolish as Mother. I shall insist upon having many helpers."

"And if your husband denies you?"

"Deny me? Why would he deny me?"

Jinny rinsed the soap out of her little brother's long pants and tried to choose her words wisely. "Perhaps he might wrongly think you are slothful."

"Slothful indeed," Owena scoffed. She sat up straight long enough to shoo a fly away from her face, and then relaxed again.

"Aye, but he might think it."

"Then I shall have to outwit him."

She hid her smile, wrung the water out of the pants, and tossed them in the basket. "That, I should like to see."

"Of course you shall see it. Did I not already say I shall not marry lest you marry as well and come with me?"

There were advantages in having her back turned to her sister, and the expression on her face made it clear that Jinny was less than pleased. She stopped what she was doing and stared at the smoke rising high above the trees from the Battie village that lay but a few miles down the main road. She could avoid her present quandary, if she were brave enough to seek a husband among the Battie, albeit over her father's objection. True, she loved her sister and might even miss her should they be separated, but it would be far from the end of the world. The end of the world would be if Kam chose Owena, Jinny wed another MacGreagor – and was forced to live in the same village.

Truly, that was a situation she simply could not, and would not abide under any circumstances.

"Did I not say that?" Owena pressed.

Jinny finished washing her other little brother's nearly worn out long pants, and began to wring them out. "Aye, Owena, but you do not say of love. Perhaps you do not wish to love your husband, but I do and if I am forced on a lad, then I shall never be happy."

"You might be happy. You might love him later."

"I would much rather love him, or at least fancy him aforehand."

"Then you prefer to marry an Allaway, for you'll not have much time to like a lad aforehand – not as long as the choosin' is left up to the lads. As well, father must be agreeable enough to give his approval, which he rarely is."

"Did Father not already give the MacGreagor permission to choose one of us?"

"Aye, but suppose father becomes disagreeable suddenly, as you know very well he is prone to do."

Jinny closed her eyes and hung her head. "Oh, I suspect when you are asked for, father shall be agreeable enough. He favors you best, you know."

Owena wrinkled her brow. "So you keep sayin', but he does not often speak or even smile at me. At you, he smiles, but rarely at me."

"He smiles at you," Jinny said, turning around to toss the wet pants in the basket and get another garment. "You just rush away before 'tis able to be seen." She frowned at the stain that forever refused to come out of her little sister's skirt, shrugged, washed, rinsed the soap out, twisted the garment to release the excess water, and tossed it in the basket. For a moment, she stood up straight, put her hands in the small of her aching back and rested. She glowered at the pile of clothes remaining, grabbed the next, and went back to work.

Still not willing to help, Owena noticed the pile of children's clothing as well. "Mother gives father too many wee ones."

Jinny took a moment to wistfully glance up at the heavens. "I hope to have six or seven, at least."

"Whatever for?"

"To hold and to love. There is nothin' I find more delightful than the soft skin of a newly come bairn. Of course, that is before they grow up to be..." She decided not to finish that sentence for she was about to say grow up like Owena.

"To be what?"

There was no point, for mentioning her sister's shortcomings always fell on deaf ears. "To be older."

"Aye, well, that cannae be helped either. If only the world would let a lass choose how many children she is to have. I wish to have none at all for they cry, they demand to be fed, and they are forever in need of someone to tend the washin.'"

"Wishin' such is useless folly. The world was already made before we were born, and no one has a say in how many children they shall have."

"Aye, but I shall wish it anyway." Owena got up, carefully walked across the rocks and headed back to the village.

Jinny watched her go. The basket would soon be too heavy for her to manage alone, but she was used to that. Long ago, she learned to take half of the wet clothes to the trees, hang them over the branches to dry, and then bring the basket back to the creek for the other half. Besides, the one thing she loved more than any other, was time alone to dream her dreams.

THAT IAN WAS CONSIDERED a misfit among the residents of the much larger Battie clan was an understatement. He was short, thin, kept his hair cropped off at the shoulders, and had yet to be considered worthy when it came to taking a wife. Attracting a wife was not the problem once he laid eyes on young Teva MacGreagor. Twice he had occasion to speak to her, while she visited a friend in the Lennox clan, and she fancied him too. No happier man lived than Ian Battie. That was before Laird MacGreagor refused to allow the marriage. The excuse for the denial was worse than weak, for Teva was certainly old enough, and short enough to make Ian a good wife. Therefore, he saw none, nor could even imagine an honorable reason for being denied.

That he was indeed denied vexed him no end.

As he rode away from the MacGreagor village, his mood turned from extreme disappointment, to anger, and then to thoughts of revenge. If there was a way to get even with the MacGreagors, he aimed to find it.

A short two months later, the answer presented itself during a casual conversation with another hunter. Kam MacGreagor, Laird MacGreagor's son, was as good as married to an Allaway. The Lennox hunter knew little more, save to hear the Allaway lass was seen as pleasing in the eyes of many a lad.

Therefore, an idea began to form in Ian's mind and he set out to see this Allaway lass for himself. Taking cover behind bushes and trees, it was not long before he discovered of which lass the Lennox had been talking. Indeed, she was the bonniest lass he had ever seen too. Day after day, he returned just so he could be witness to the day Kam came to take his bride. Twice he openly came to the village on the pretense of having something to barter, but although she was there, and was pleasant enough to him, she gave him not a second look. He was not insulted for his eyes were only for Teva. All he had to do was wait. Time would give Teva to him – he was certain of it.

That he was not often noticed missing by his clan bothered him not. No one asked when he returned, for he was a hunter, having the usual good and bad days on the hunt. His size gave him the only advantage, for he could discover rabbits hiding under bushes far easier than the larger men.

On this day, instead of going into the Allaway village, he was once more content to watch the sisters from a hiding place inside the forest. The more he saw of the bonnie one, the more he began to think of ways he could approach her – things he could offer her to entice her away, and thereby avoid any sort of major confrontation. It would not do to get caught before he was in a position to trade her for his beloved Teva.

It was while Owena sunned herself on the rock, that he got near enough to hear what was said.

"Owena," he muttered. "She is called Owena." He watched her shoo away another fly before he remembered that it had been days since he took meat back to the clan. As soon as Owena left, he quietly slipped back through the forest to his horse, and set out to find some measure of game to take home, even if it was just a rabbit or two.

He might miss the happy event, but he knew what Owena looked like and even now knew her name. It was a good sign that all was going precisely as he hoped.

NEARLY A WEEK HAD PASSED by the time the brothers began to put more effort into the cottages they were building. Having little room left for more cottages on the flat land, the men had worked tirelessly the winter before to fell the trees and level two patches of ground side by side, atop a slight incline that overlooked most of the village and a good portion of the loch.

Glendon, the brother who had slept beside Kam since he was born, liked his brother in spite of the constant bickering that usually led to some sort of physical challenge. Apparently, there were things about Glendon that Kam found irritating. Mostly, Glendon supposed, it was because he had a way of outwitting Kam.

In size and brute strength, the brothers were equals, but their likeness went no farther. Though he was quiet and more observant, the MacGreagor women often commented on how good it was that Glendon was the younger, for he was often too kind, and even Kam had to admit it was true. Kam, on the other hand, was to be the next laird, and everyone said he was stern enough to make him well suited for the task. Glendon was never quite convinced. He felt his brother a little too unpredictable to lead the people well. Besides, being kind was not exactly a major transgression, not to his way of thinking. Even so, Kam was the eldest and to him would go the honor of being the next laird.

Both brothers listened when their mother tried to instruct them in the ways of husbands and wives, and each came away with a different impression. Being stern, she told Kam, was not all that becoming to an unmarried lass, and for him to attract her, he must let his soft side show more. It greatly perplexed Kam, Glendon noticed, for he understood not how to be anything other than what he truly was. Her advice to Glendon was not to be overly kind, for a wife must see his strength to feel safe when the days of great turmoil arrive. Of course, never had he seen days of great turmoil, and could not quite grasp her meaning. He would learn, Glendon supposed.

As to their chores, both preferred being outside rather than inside even when it rained. It was especially true on fine spring days, during which they were forced to work on their cottages. Outside, the birds happily chirped, the dogs were chasing rabbits, and even Calla's annoying and constant bray was better than being inside.

That morning, Glendon stepped through the doorway of his cottage and took a moment to look around just to see what still needed to be done. He longed for more windows, but more than one window would not only let in the winter cold, it would be more dangerous should they ever be attacked.

Kam was already complaining that he feared he would not finish his cottage first, which meant that Glendon would win Owena's hand. After a week, Glendon was sick of hearing it. However, he had not changed his mind, and if anything, Kam's complaining made him more determined to win.

Kam had been neglectful in his building, had fallen far behind, and deserved to lose.

Glendon went back outside, looked for his brother and when he did not see him, he went into Kam's cottage. That their cottages were next to each other was not by choice – it just turned out that way. Instead of two stools, which were harder and more time consuming to make, Kam settled for a bench long enough for two, and thought that plenty good enough. His bench was a little wobbly, but it would do. He managed, Glendon noted, to make a higher, and far longer bench to put against the wall for a wife to fix his meals on, and to store bowls, spoons and food. That just left a bed to make. As far as he was concerned, a mattress on the floor suited Kam just fine, but their mother insisted no daughter-in-law of hers was to sleep on the floor. She demanded a box that was at least a foot high to set her mattress on.

Glendon had just stepped out of Kam's cottage when his brother started up the incline.

Kam shrugged and went to the pile of wood to choose four short boards of equal length with which to make legs for his table. Next, he set those aside, chose another piece of wood, took a seat on a log, and began to carve the wooden pegs necessary to hold the table and legs together. He tried his best to ignore his brother, who was about to put his table together. "You be nearly finished, I suppose," Kam said.

"Nearly." Glendon picked up a wooden hammer and began to drive the pegs he'd carved the day before, through the top of the square table into each leg. Finished, he then tested the table on the flat land in front of the cottages to make certain it was sturdy and level. Pleased with his work, he could not help but smile.

Kam had an obvious glower on his face when he said, "You've already made a box bed?"

"Aye, yesterday, and I fully intend to sleep on it this very night." Glendon picked up the table and carried it inside his cottage.

"At least I have a door," Kam sneered when his brother came back out. "Wives insist on doors, you know."

"*My* wife shall surely desire one, for I shall tell her to keep well away from you."

Kam shot back, "Have you not often said you are too young to marry?"

"Have I? Nay, I dinna recall havin' said it – leastwise not often."

"You changed your mind simply to claim Owena, and about that you lied. You have not seen her."

"Then how is it I know her name?"

"You must have heard me speak of her in my sleep, for she is constantly on my mind."

"Nay, I heard of her when last I went huntin', which was before you last went just as I said. The Allaway hunters told me about her, so I had a look for myself."

"You went to the village?" a disbelieving Kam asked.

"Nay, I saw her from afar."

"Why did you not say you wanted to marry her as soon as you saw her?"

Glendon paused to think of a good answer. "She be a bit young still?"

"You mean; *you* be a bit young still!"

"That too."

"And now you think you are not? I find folly in that."

Glendon could not help but raise his voice. "You would!"

"Next, you shall say you love her."

"Nay, I dinna love her, not yet. Nevertheless, I shall finish my cottage first, father will declare me the winner, and then I shall have her and not you." Glendon chose the four flat boards with which to build a door, and laid them side-by-side on the ground. He decided he did not have enough pegs to do the job properly, sat down not far from his brother at the woodpile, and pulled out his knife. "Did you not say Owena has a sister?"

"Aye, and she is just as bonnie, perhaps even more so."

Glendon turned to stare at his brother. "Now who lies? If she were more so, you would prefer her and not Owena."

"And if I did, you would prefer Jinny instead too," Kam returned, his voice raising as well. "Admit it, you have always wanted what pleases me most."

"Everythin' and everyone pleases you most. You cannae have the whole loaf of bread and leave the crumbs for me. Not this time, not when it comes to choosin' a wife." Disgusted, Glendon grabbed his wood, got up and started to walk down the incline.

"Fear not, Owena shall prefer me over you," Kam shouted after him.

Glendon abruptly stopped and turned around. "You cannae know that, and lest you forget - a MacGreagor dinna force a lass to marry against her will, even if her father gives permission."

"And a pity that is too. A lad must make a home for her, he must feed and clothe her, and yet she is the one to decide who she shall have? 'Tis rearward, and you know it."

"I know nothin' of the sort. I dinna want a wife who dinna prefer me as well."

Kam again scoffed, "She already prefers me. I saw her up close and 'twas in her eyes. And, whilst I was there, her father bid *me* to choose between Owena and her sister."

"You chose Owena?"

Kam dropped his angry expression and looked down. "Nay, I said I had not father's permission, but I promised to go back and choose. When I do, I shall choose Owena."

"She is likely already claimed."

"Nay, she waits. Laird Allaway wishes his daughter, rather both of his daughters, to marry a MacGreagor."

"Why?"

"Because he finds fault with the other clans on our side of the loch, and his wife wishes for an easy visit."

Glendon folded his arms and persisted. "And what else?"

"Nothin' else, that be the reason."

"Why do I think there is more? Perhaps 'tis the pleased look on your face when you know somethin' you wish me not to know?"

"Believe what you will. It matters not to me."

Completely disgusted with his brother's part of the conversation, Glendon went back, grabbed two pieces of wood, walked down the incline, and then up to the top of the hill.

Kam watched him go and then hung his head. "I should not have told Laird Allaway I would bring a brother."

IF THERE WAS A THING happening, Cerdic was usually the first to know, for he was constantly where he ought not to be. A boy of eleven who thought himself nearly grown was the curious sort, and feared not the repercussions of his actions. He would be in big trouble if his father knew he was not tending the sheep as he was supposed to be. However, it would not be the first time he'd been sent to Ronson MacGreagor to admit his shortcomings, and endure a stern talking to. He could hear it all now – 'everyone must work, and then everyone may seek their pleasure. 'Tis the way of the world.' They were the same words his father often said as well.

Cerdic learned long ago that not all people, even MacGreagors, were always truthful all the time. It was up to him to decide who was being honest and who was not. The way he saw it, he could not rightly judge people unless he was where he could hear what they were talking about. Therefore, when Kam and Glendon were sitting outside in front of their cottages, Cerdic simply happened to be there, leaning against a tree where the brothers were unlikely to spot him.

The truth was, tending the sheep was Cerdic's least favorite chore in all the world. It meant he was rarely party to what was happening in the village. He was not there when Rossalyn climbed the hill in the pouring rain, slipped, and slid all the way down on her backside. He surely would have liked seeing that instead of just hearing about it being such a sight to be seen from the others. There was always something fascinating to watch in the village, and if not, he was always guaranteed entertainment when Kam and Glendon went at it. Rain, snow or heat of day – nothing stopped the bickering between the laird's sons.

Cerdic had secrets too, things he'd seen that he never told a soul, but those were few and far between. He supposed everyone did, and they weren't talking either, but they hadn't heard what he just heard. Although everyone already knew the brothers desired the same wife, they did not know that Kam told Laird Allaway he had a brother – but what did it matter? Cerdic scratched his head in bewilderment. He waited until Kam was not looking before he slipped away and went to ponder the situation.

He could tell the others what was said and ask their opinion, if he had a mind to, but normally, he liked knowing the answer before he told a thing. Yet, for the life of him, he could not think why it was significant. Did everyone not already know Kam had a brother? Everyone he knew was aware of it, but it appeared Laird Allaway did not, and perhaps his daughters did not know either. Still, Kam mentioned it, so it must be of grave importance.

Abruptly, his eyes widened. Did Kam not say Laird Allaway has *two* daughters? Indeed he did, and claimed the other was just as bonnie. Cerdic was only eleven years of age, but even he could see that two men were necessary if Laird Allaway wished his daughters to marry MacGreagors. He pondered the idea of rushing off to tell everyone, but then he gave it more thought. Instead, he decided to follow the brothers, and himself be witness to which married the favored Owena. It was possible Owena might deny both Kam and Glendon. Therefore, it might also be his only chance to get a good look at two remarkably bonnie lasses, before he was put upon to take a wife of his own.

ON THE CREST OF THE hill was always a good place for Glendon to do his whittling, the sunshine was warm, blooming wild flowers enhanced the beauty of the glen, and most of all there was no brother nearby to annoy him. Like his father, peace and quiet always calmed his irritation, and just now he needed to calm down so he could return to the work of finishing his cottage. Otherwise, Kam would win. Perhaps his brother's hidden intention was to irritate Glendon and therefore delay his work. That was it, probably. Then again, it occurred to him there was something more to be concerned about. Kam always had a way of getting Glendon to change his mind, and that was likely what he was up to now. But what? What could Kam possibly say that would convince Glendon to give Owena up? Nothing, Glendon decided. He desired her and nothing could tempt him otherwise.

CHAPTER 5

WHEN TWO OF THE ALLAWAY men were set to take several items they wished to barter with the Lennox, Jinny asked to go with them. That very morning she decided she needed to see more of the world. If Kam did not choose her, then perhaps she might find a husband among the Lennox, providing they did not live all that close to the MacGreagors, where Owena might live. What she longed for most was a few hours away from Owena.

"Nay daughter," said Laird Allaway at first. He stood near the vast vegetable garden, overseeing the work of the women, who's chore it was to pull weeds and carry buckets of water from the creek. It was so early in the spring some of the vegetables had not yet had time to sprout, therefore the weeds were easier to see.

"But father, rarely do you allow me to..."

"'Tis not safe," he interrupted. "There," he said, pointing at a particular weed. The woman nearest him frowned.

Nevertheless, the woman stood up straight, rubbed her aching back, and then took her hoe to the weed. "I say let them both go," she suggested, though she did not look at Laird Allaway or Jinny when she said it.

Laird Allaway rubbed the stubble on his unshaven chin. "Both?" He considered that for a moment. "Indeed, let Owena go as well. 'Twill be pleasant for them both."

Aye, pleasant for you, a disturbed Jinny almost said. She looked around for her sister and as usual, found her not to be outside. Why would she be? Outside, her father might try to put Owena to work. She looked at the woman who suggested it, but the woman had her head down and would not look Jinny in the eye. Her only hope at that point was if Owena refused to go. It was possible, Jinny supposed, for her sister never wanted to go anywhere.

"O WENA!" her father yelled. Slow as always, it took time for Owena to finally appear in the doorway of the Laird's cottage. "Jinny wishes to go with the lads to the Lennox village, and you are to go with her!"

It was a command, not a request, and normally Owena did and said all manner of things to resist her father's commands. This time, however, she did not readily answer and instead looked as if she was actually contemplating it.

Jinny stared at her sister and held her breath.

"Aye Father," Owena said. She darted back inside without noticing the obvious disapproval in Jinny's expression.

Jinny moaned. "Must I go with her?"

Laird Allaway seemed genuinely surprised. "You have changed your mind?"

She put the back of her hand on her forehead. "I fear a headache shall soon consume all of my good humor."

"Oh, is that all?" He chuckled. "Well then, a ride in the fresh air shall do you very good indeed."

She was stuck and there was no way out. Of all his children, he appreciated Jinny most, or so he often said when the two of them were alone. It was not hard to see why, because it was usually Jinny who kept Owena occupied. Her mother helped on days when Owena refused to leave the cottage, but mostly, it was left up to Jinny. He needed his solitude, or so he emphatically always stated. She needed hers too, but her needs never exceeded his. Oh well, there was nothing to be done, short of marrying the first lad who asked for her. Hopefully, that would be Kam MacGreagor.

It took time for Owena to get ready to go. The men soon became agitated, and Laird Allaway commanded that two more warriors assist them in keeping his beloved daughters safe. Now there were four men in waiting, all looking just as frustrated as Jinny felt. At least they looked kindly on her, for they fully understood the misery that was her life.

THE ALLAWAY WERE WELL received in the Lennox village, especially Owena, and when she asked in which direction they should go to see the lightning tree, several men offered to show her. Owena laughed. She always laughed when she needed time to think of an excuse, and then assure them no Allaway had ever gotten lost, and she intended not to be the first. Jinny thought the idea of Owena getting lost was a fine one, but although the men were disappointed, they let Owena have her way. Jinny was not surprised. Silly men always let Owena have her way.

It turned out that the Lennox village, although located around a natural bend in the loch, was not that far from the MacGreagor village. Instead of walking with her sister, Jinny stayed far behind, hoping not to be noticed by the MacGreagors. However, and to Jinny's relief, as soon as they got close to the stone wall, Owena darted behind a clump of bushes.

For a moment, Jinny considered staying out in the open, but she soon changed her mind less Kam see her. It would not bode well for him to think she came to spy on the man she hoped to marry. No indeed, she would not like him to have any reason at all to think ill of her, so she joined her sister behind the bushes.

The lightning tree was much bigger than she imagined, and just as was said, it bore the black mark of a lightning strike. Three of the lower branches remained, although they grew no more and the top of the tree was completely gone. At least, she had seen it for herself and feared it not. It was just a tree.

If Owena noticed it, she did not say. Instead, both of them turned to look when a mule suddenly began to bray. Both girls covered their mouths to muffle their laughter when they spotted the mule sitting near the edge of the forest, refusing to budge even though one of the men had a rope around its neck, pulling and insisting it get up.

It was then Jinny spotted Kam and felt her heart flutter, just the way it had the day she met him. He carried something up an incline and then disappeared inside one of two cottages. She hoped Owena had not seen him and never would, but that dinna last long. Just as quickly as he went in, he came back out, stood in front of the cottage and then rubbed one of his arms. He seemed to be looking for someone, or perhaps something more to take inside, and Owena was definitely watching him too.

"Are not all the MacGreagor lads handsome?" Jinny whispered, hoping to distract her sister.

Owena lifted her chin. "They look the same as any other lads to me, although perhaps taller."

As soon as Kam went into the forest, Jinny watched the other men tend to their various chores, but she watched the women too and wrinkled her brow. She was in wonder at how happily they went about their work. None of them were made to weed the garden. In fact, the men tended to that chore, and they did not appear to need anyone to tell them where the weeds were.

She was greatly perplexed. Although the Allaway women worked just as hard, they were anything but jovial in the doing. Right then, one of the MacGreagors started to sing and soon, the villagers joined in. There were rumors about the odd way the MacGreagors treated women, for most men were very demanding of their wives. The Allaway were, and so were the MacKellar and the Lennox. She knew little of the

Battie. The rumors, she heard, were mostly spread by the Lennox, and Jinny always supposed the Lennox were mistaken. Now, she was not so sure. If the rumors of their good nature were true, so also might the one about a curse be true.

Still, how could it be that a cursed clan so skillfully gave the appearance of being joyful?

More often than not, daughters were betrothed to men they did not like or had not even met. It was the way of clans, the fathers knowing what was best, or so fathers claimed. A daughter could raise the standing of a clan if she was given in marriage, or could be traded for livestock, land or even jewels. Such arrangements were made without the knowledge of the bride-to-be, but women talked the same as men. The Allaway girls knew – all the girls old enough to marry knew.

She was at least grateful her father had not done such as that to her, at least not yet.

"Kam builds a new cottage," Jinny said, tired of squatting and finally stepping out from behind the bushes. At the moment she was no longer concerned about what Kam might think of her if he saw her. "'Tis a sure sign he means to choose a wife soon. I wonder who the other new cottage might be for?"

Owena stepped out from behind the bushes too and scoffed, "I wonder that we have even come. I shall not have a MacGreagor." This time, Owena had not been as careful when it came to her manner of dress. It was muggy out and she hadn't bothered to finish tying her wool vest. Instead, she left it half open and let the strings hang loosely down the front of her skirt. As well, the top clasp on her shirt was open. That was embarrassing for Jinny, but normal for Owena.

It was Jinny who cared to wear a soft leather vest over her most presentable full length frock, and a shirt with long sleeves tied with string at the wrist. She turned to look at her sister. "'Tis not what you said yesterday."

"Yesterday, I was young and foolish. Today I am older and far too wise to prefer a MacGreagor."

Jinny snickered, "Aye, a whole day older."

Owena ignored her. "Their village be too small, less than half the size of ours, and they are too near the loch. No doubt they are flooded out come the autumn rains." She brushed dirt off her skirt, and then looked to see if she had attracted the attention of any of the MacGreagors. She hadn't. "Oh, I shall accept Kam if Father thinks it a good match, but Kam is much too tall."

"Too tall for what?"

"Dear one, sometimes wisdom escapes you. Beds are never long enough for a tall man. Therefore, in an effort to keep his feet warm, he must curl up, which leaves little room in his bed for a wife."

Jinny wrinkled her brow. "I had not thought of that."

"I much prefer a Lennox instead." Owena sighed. She looked toward the neighboring Lennox village, but could see neither the village nor any of the men who had previously admired her. The only man near enough to see was an elder sheep herder. "Shall we not go home? I tire. I would rather see the Lennox than the MacGreagors."

"Very well." Jinny glanced once more at the MacGreagor village, still could not see Kam, and followed Owena down the path toward where the Lennox lived. "I dinna prefer a Lennox, not one I saw, leastwise."

"A MacKellar then?"

"Perhaps. I did see one MacKellar I thought handsome when last they came to barter with us."

"Aye, but I found the way he looked at me quite unworthy. I do hope he shall not soon come back." Owena abruptly stopped and turned around to look her sister in the eye. "You dinna imagine Father has betrothed me to the MacKellar, do you? I mean, I'd not like livin' so far away from mother."

"I hardly think Father would discuss such a thing with me. Besides, did he not promise one of us to Kam MacGreagor."

Owena again sighed, turned back around and started down the path again. "Or Mother. He tells her very little."

"I would wish my husband to tell me everythin'."

"That's not likely. Mother often complains of that particular circumstance, and still she does not know a thing until it has long since passed. Why Father does not speak of it to her, I know not."

"They tell other lads right enough," Jinny pointed out, "but from us, the world is some sort of well-guarded secret."

"But why?"

Jinny shrugged, and then grabbed the side of her skirt to keep it from getting caught on a bush. "Because they think we are too skittish to know what they know. I find it maddenin'."

"Perhaps we *are* too skittish?"

"Perhaps *you* are," Jinny said, "but I am not. I hunger for knowledge, for sights and all manner of sounds. Why a lass is not allowed to go with the lads when they journey is beyond my understandin'. 'Tis not fair."

Owena only sighed. "Father let us come today."

There was plenty Jinny could, and desperately wanted to say to that, but she let it pass. "Aye."

"And I am glad. I know now I must refuse to marry a MacGreagor. Mistress of such a small clan is the same as bein' no mistress at all."

Jinny did not believe her. Why should she? Owena had changed her mind often in the past, too often to keep up with her whimsical fancies on some days. Still, there was a slight glimmer of hope that this time her sister was being truthful. As soon as they reached the Lennox village, Owena was instantly greeted by gawking, overly attentive men. It was enough to make Jinny nauseous, and she was glad when a girl her age befriended her. She went with her new friend to see a new litter of puppies born just that morning, and it served to cheer her up. Her new friendship was short-lived, however, when the Allaway men brought the horses, helped both Owena and Jinny mount, and then took them home.

Perhaps tomorrow Kam would come to take her away. It was what Jinny wished most. She wished it with all her heart.

STANDING IN THE MIDDLE of Kam's cottage, Laird Ronson MacGreagor thoughtfully rocked from heel to toe and back again. His hands were clasped behind his back, his eyes were fixed on the one and only sitting bench, and his brow was wrinkled. "You mean to stand while eatin'?"

"Nay, 'tis room for two on the bench," Kam answered.

"I see." Ronson said nothing more, and made no mention of it when he noticed Kam's table was a bit lopsided, and he had yet to build a taller bench along the wall for storage and food preparation. No bucket did he see, no bowls and no spoons. Next, he nodded his approval at the way the box had been made, upon which the mattress would lay, and then unclasped his hand and examined the door. At least the door exhibited the workmanship Kam had been taught.

With that, Ronson walked out and went to see the inside of Glendon's cottage. He said nothing of Glendon's work either, and simply went about the rest of his day.

Early the next morning, Ronson came down from his favorite place on the hill and let it be known there was to be a celebration that night. The MacGreagors were delighted as well as intrigued, for a spring celebration could only mean one thing – it was tradition after all, for the laird to give permission for the MacGreagor sons and daughters to marry.

Just twice a year did the MacGreagors pause in their daily lives to celebrate. Naturally, a feast was called for after the exhaustive work of gleaning the autumn harvest, cleaning the vegetables, drying the seeds, and storing the winter provisions in the cellars. The second cause for celebration came after the long winter when spring lightened everyone's step, the bushes brought forth wild berries, and the bright green leaves seemingly sprang forth overnight from sleeping trees. Rabbits peeked out from behind bushes as though to show off their latest litter, mud puddles from countless drops of rain dried up, and children were more often let out to play.

Because there was no particular day marked for the spring celebration, it was up to the laird to proclaim the day. By noon, six fathers had approached him, asking to be heard on behalf of a son or daughter. It was not as if the fathers could not ask any time during the year, but having the laird's blessing at the spring celebration was special. It promised that the marriage would be happy and fruitful, or so everyone believed.

Inside the MacGreagor great hall; the largest room of any in the village, Ronson sat at the head of a long table. Three candles that had been placed in a row down the center of the table, added to the light of a large hearth. It was not where Ronson liked spending his time. The chair was uncomfortable, he found being so far away from those at the other end of the room annoying, and seemed always to be asking them to speak up.

On this occasion it was necessary. Deciding if a little one, who had somehow miraculously grown up before his very eyes should marry, always tore at his heart, especially when it came to the young women. A warm and gentle man, his arms were always open to the little ones, in which he greatly delighted. Perhaps knowing the children so very well was the reason that allowing a union between a man and woman gave Ronson the most pause.

He listened to the pleas of four and then five fathers, appropriately pausing after, as if to give the decision careful consideration. Always before, he agreed in the end, unless he thought the lad unworthy, be he a MacGreagor or from another clan. When it came to the wishes of his young men, Ronson encouraged intermarriage with the other clans, for wives became MacGreagors and increased the size of the clan. Allowing a young woman to marry and become a member of her husband's clan was far more grievous to his way of thinking. That meant a decrease in the clan. It was hard enough losing members to illness or injury, but to give one away in marriage pained Ronson.

It was for that reason that he was inclined to forbid the marriage of Thomas MacGreagor's youngest daughter to a MacKellar. She was old enough, but he imagined her too soft hearted to endure a life in a warring clan. The truth be told, he felt the same about all young MacGreagor women.

"But I love him," the hopeful bride insisted, "and he loves me."

"Love?" Ronson asked. "Can one so young and tender truly know of love?" Yet, when he glanced at Thomas, one of his trusted defenders, and noticed the chagrin on his face, he reconsidered. "Shall you come to us instead if there is to be a battle."

"I give you my pledge," the bride promised.

"Aye, then, if 'twill please you, I give my permission. Ronson watched the happy father and daughter leave his home, and then stood up. That was the last of them, and he had more important things to do.

Yet, there was one marriage denial that bothered him still, though he had yet to change his mind. When Ian Battie came to ask for Teva, word had already been heard that Ian was not exactly a teller of truth. Lying was not seen as the worst of crimes, but a wife, especially the straight minded Teva, would soon grow weary of such a fallacy. Furthermore, when Teva hesitated to agree to the marriage, Ronson took it to mean she did not truly prefer Ian.

What bothered him was an omission of honesty on his part. His excuse at the time seemed valid enough – he did not wish to break the young man's heart. Still, he would have done better had he pointed out her unwillingness, and thereby setting Ian free to find another. Ronson sighed. There was likely nothing he could do about it now, so he went outside to enjoy a meal with the rest of the clan.

The mood was more than jovial with laughter, cheering, and refilled cups, although Kam seemed a little distraught. That was to be expected. When Ronson finished eating, he asked to speak to his sons alone.

He considered sitting again in the most uncomfortable chair in the world at the head of the table, and instead started up the hill with Kam and Glendon following. The last rays of sunlight had cast a pink and purple glow on a smattering of clouds that hung over the mountains to the west, the world was about to go to sleep for the night, and save for some laughter in the village, he was greeted with a peaceful calm.

"When we spoke last of takin' a wife, both of you desired to marry the same lass. It that your desire still?" Ronson asked, folding his arms as he usually did.

"Aye," Kam said while Glendon nodded his answer. Both of them folded their arms as well, although Glendon glanced more often at the beautiful sunset than did his brother.

"I see. I shall allow Glendon first choice of a wife." He expected Kam to argue, but he did not. A perplexed Ronson asked his eldest son, "You find my decision pleasin'?"

"Pleasin'? Nay, Father, pleasin' 'twould be a lie. All I ask is that I be allowed to go with him when he asks for Owena."

Ronson turned his attention to Glendon. "Have you an objection?"

"Nay Father, I cannae wait to see what he is up to." Glendon snickered when Kam rolled his eyes.

"Very well then, I have spoken it." He shifted his full weight to the other foot. "Both of you have my permission to marry, but first I am inclined to say what must be said in the matter of takin' a wife."

"Father, we are grown. We know what must be done," Glendon offered.

Kam, Ronson noticed, appeared to be bored. "Do you?" he asked Glendon. "I think not. Many a lad has been made unhappy because he chose unwisely. I charge you not to choose a lass in haste. Betroth her first if you are inclined, and then see her once or twice before you marry, thereby learnin' more about her. If she does not please you, then you save yourself the trouble of bein' married to her forever."

"What is there to learn?" Glendon wanted to know.

"Well, you may ask of her health and such things that are ordinary to MacGreagors, but not so in other clans. Learn if her laughter pleases you. Is she kind? Moreover, will she please your mother?"

"Mother?" Kam asked. "What has Mother to do with it?"

"Much," Ronson answered. "If your mother cannae abide her, well...you have seen it. My wife tolerates those she dinna like, but she hides not her disapproval."

"Oh," said Kam. "You are right about that much at least."

"At least?" Ronson asked. "I fear you hear me not, son. Life is not long enough with the right wife, and too long when a lad marries wrongly."

Kam's grin began to widen. "I shall know my wife at least as long as you knew mother before you married her."

Ronson took a deep frustrated breath. "'Twas not the same."

"How?" Kam pressed. "Did you not say you loved her from the moment you laid eyes upon her? And does she not say the same of you? Were you not married that very day, and..."

"Aye, but I was more fortunate than many a lad. Happiness is not won as in battle, nor 'tis it given or taken." Ronson glanced up at the dimming sunset. "You know to help her when a thing be too heavy, to protect her and to pick her up when she falls, but do you know how to please a lass when she is your wife?"

"Please her," Kam scoffed. "My wife shall be pleased for she shall want for nothin'. I shall..."

"Please her how, Father?" Glendon interrupted.

Ronson was relieved to be talking to someone with a little more sense about such things. "If you are wise and learn about her before you marry, then you shall know how to please her."

"Forgive me, Father, but I've a thing to do," said Kam finally.

When his eldest son abruptly turned and headed down the hill, Ronson shook his head. He watched Kam walk to his unfinished cottage, go inside and close the door. "Glendon, I hope you have learned not to be as hasty as your brother."

"I have, Father."

"I pray so, but one thing more, a man with a wife does not fight his brother, even if 'tis only practice. He must not take the chance of gettin' hurt, and therefore be unable to protect her if needs be." He paused to give his son a moment to think that over. "Shall you leave in the mornin'?"

"Aye."

Ronson put a hand on his son's shoulder. "Take care you come back safely."

Glendon nodded. "I shall, Father."

"Good, then we best get on with it." When Glendon started down the hill, Ronson followed him.

CHAPTER 6

IN THE GLOW OF THE larger than usual fire, the people in the MacGreagor village stood by, happily anticipating the giving of the sword. Everyone knew Ronson would present it to Kam, for he was the eldest son, but there was a slight possibility their laird might hand the sword to Glendon instead. It was not unheard of for a laird to bypass the eldest in cases of illness, or unable to take on the responsibility in some other way. In any event, it was a reason to celebrate, and never did a MacGreagor turn down a reason to celebrate.

The women tried to keep their youngest children in tow, and puppies managed to chase each other, darting in and out of the people, while some of the older children chased after the dogs. In the light of the fire, the people looked healthy, happy and contented just to be MacGreagors.

When Ronson and Glendon came down the hill without Kam, the people wondered if perchance their laird had indeed chosen his second son to lead them. To some, that would seem right. To others, it was unthinkable, and the rest cared little one way or the other.

Ronson searched the crowd for his eldest son, and when he did not set eyes on him, he shouted, "Kam!"

"Here, Father," Kam answered. The people parted to let him pass, and soon he stood in front of his father.

From the sheath he had worn since his father presented it to him, Ronson pulled out the sword. He held it straight up, and then raised it high enough for all to see. "Kam, I choose you to lead the clan whence I am gone from this earth.

Appropriately, Kam bowed his head. "Aye, Father."

"You are charged with seein' to the needs of your people," Ronson continued, "to judge them with fair-minded discernment when somethin' is amiss, and to lead them in battle should the need arise. Furthermore, you are to take every precaution to keep them out of battle, and particular care where the lasses and the children are concerned." He paused to take a deep breath. "Do you agree to wear the sword with honor, and to abide by the edict handed down from your forefathers?"

"I do, Father," Kam answered.

Ronson's hesitation was brief, but did not go unnoticed. "If that be the case, then I name you the next MacGreagor laird."

It was only then that Kam smiled, and as was the custom, he knelt before Ronson and bowed his head.

In return, Ronson bid him to rise. He handed the sword to Kam, untied the strings that bound the sheath to him, and then tied them around his son's waist instead. When he was finished, he stood back. "May a blessin' be upon you, my son."

To the cheers of the people, Kam lowered the sword and put it in its sheath. Not everyone was exuberantly gleeful, but they held any hint of discontent from Ronson and instead shared a brief knowing glance with someone else. Among those was Ronson's twin sister, Rossalyn. But then, Rossalyn never hid her opinions from anyone, especially her brother.

As soon as Kam turned to stand next to his father, the men came to honor him with a pledge to obey, and a nod of the head. Even the boy children came, which delighted their parents – for they wished the tradition to continue, and they were well aware few in the oldest generation would live long enough to see another sword presentation.

After the formal ceremony was ended and each drank a cup of ale, it was Rossalyn who asked Ronson what all of them wondered. "Why do you pass the sword now? Are you unwell?"

Ronson leaned forward and touched his cheek to hers. "I'd not depend upon my leavin' you behind any time soon, if I were you."

Rossalyn grinned. "I am pleased to hear it."

It was then the flute player began a jig and it was then that, instead of dancing with his wife, Ronson danced the first jig with his sister. While he seemed not to tire in the least, she soon no longer favored such a fast dance, and gave up her place to Ronson's wife, Mayzie. Rossalyn was thereby convinced they would not see the end of Ronson for some years yet, and so was everyone else.

Instead, Rossalyn went to join her husband, Birk. Theirs had been a long and happy marriage with six children, two of which yet lived. William was their eldest and knew both Kam and Glendon better than anyone else.

As he often did, Birk took his wife's hand, and together they walked down the path that led to their cottage. Once they were well away from the others, he said, "Glendon looked pleased."

"Because he was not chosen to be the next laird?" Rossalyn asked.

"That perhaps, but I suspect Ronson gave Glendon first choice of whom to marry."

"Then 'tis true what everyone says? The brothers desire the same lass?"

"Aye, 'tis what William said, and so does Cerdic. Cerdic heard Kam and Glendon talkin' of her whilst they were finishin' their cottages."

Rossalyn abruptly stopped walking. "They shall fight again, and this time in earnest?"

"Perhaps, but I shan't fret over it. Kam may not be the cleverest amongst us, but he is not daft. He shall surely not give up his future for a lass, and if he truly harmed his brother, Ronson would banish him."

"I hope you are right, for I have always favored Glendon." With his urging, they began to walk the path again. "What do we know of this lass?"

"She is an Allaway."

"And does she know of the MacGreagor curse?"

"Her sister knows, so 'tis likely common knowledge."

Rossalyn looked suddenly hopeful. "Then perhaps she shall deny both Kam and Glendon."

"And if not, we shall welcome Glendon's bride..."

"But husband, I dinna wish to see Kam suffer, and should she agree to marry Glendon, then Kam may well be intolerable."

"For a time perhaps." When they reached the cottage, Birk lifted the latch and opened the door. "Just now, we are alone."

She could not help but smile at the sparkle in his eye, and hurried inside to light a candle. As he always did when he wished to be alone with his wife, Birk closed the door, and then lowered the heavy board into its holder on the inside. In the scant light of the candle little could be seen of their embrace, and all that could be heard was Rossalyn's giggle.

IN THE ALLAWAY VILLAGE, it was long since known that the elders had much to say, but did not always share what they knew. For that reason, Jinny often hid near a cottage, and then followed at a respectable distance, when two particular elders went for their noon walk. Unfortunately, Owena could not be gotten rid of that afternoon, no matter what Jinny suggested her sister might find pleasing instead.

Both born into the Allaway clan, the elders Tavish and Dallis were rarely apart now that both had lost their mates. Tavish's wife died the year before when the last deadly fever swept through Scotland, and he often implied he would be asking Dallis to marry him someday. It just had not seemed to be the right time. He was a worker of metal, forging and bending the iron strips that held the wooden buckets together, making new weapons, repairing old ones, and making cooking pots. Never did a clan that size have enough flat pans or cooking pots. He liked the work, he liked his life, and he especially liked Dallis.

Dallis lost her husband when he was thrown from a horse. Promptly and without hesitation, Dallis shot an arrow into the heart of the horse, killing it instantly. For that, she faced scorn from the clan, having deprived them of a much needed animal, but to her way of thinking, the horse deserved to die for killing her husband. That was some years ago, and she had long since been forgiven.

Dallis was a worker of heather, an abundance of which grew on the hillsides. From the sturdy plant, she made pot scrubbers, rope, brooms, small berry baskets, and larger ones with leather straps in which to haul the washing to the creek. She also constructed smaller, deeper, and square rather than round baskets, a pair of which could be tied a length apart, and then lay over a horse's back. They were perfect for carrying all manner of supplies.

To say she was not an asset to the clan would be amiss, especially since she was willing to teach the newer generations, but even Dallis needed rest from her daily endeavors. Her hands were scarred and callused, and at nearly thirty, she tired more easily than she had in the past. Her hair had turned white, from lack of sleep she was told, but Dallis believed it not. Sleep never had been and was not now a problem. In fact, she could sleep sitting up when she needed to. No, she was simply getting old. It happened to everyone and she was no exception.

"You may come out now," Tavish said, standing on the path that led to her cottage.

"I shall come out when I am of a mind to," Dallis grumbled.

Tavish frowned just as he always did when she was being stubborn. "As you wish." He folded his arms in a huff, which made the thin metal strips hanging from his belt jingle.

She finally opened her door, quickly closed it behind her, and then grinned at him. "My, but are you not a handsome lad this day."

"Flattery, always with the flattery, Dallis. Have you nothin' more important to say?"

She let her grin fade. "Not today. Today I've a question."

"A question?" Tavish did not hide his suspicious expression. "Trickery, no doubt."

"Trickery? Nay, tis but a simple question even you can answer."

He more tightly folded his arms as if to brace himself for what surely was to come. Dallis had a way of twisting his words which, since he could not always remember precisely what he said, served to confuse him. "Very well, what is it?"

"Which shall the MacGreagor choose to wed – Owena or Jinny?"

"Lass, how am I to know such things? You would do better to ask the MacGreagor, if he comes back. 'Tis he who shall do the choosin'."

"You are very handsome, but a bit on the forgetful side. Who was it that chose a wife for you?"

"I'll have you know I chose my own wife."

Dallis rolled her eyes. "Think back on it. Had you no help in the choosin' – no help at all?"

"Nay, I knew the moment I saw her..."

"And was she alone when you saw her?"

He dropped his gaze and searched his memory. "Aye, she was alone."

"Was it not spring, with flowers all a bloom and the wind in her hair? Was her hair not long and unbound, her cheeks the color of a rose bud, and her clothin' clean? Did her eyes not sparkle in the sunlight when, at last, she looked up?"

The wrinkles in his forehead were deeper than even he thought possible. "How...Dallis, to whom have you been speakin'?"

"To whom would I speak? They are all dead save you and me." When she began to stroll toward the creek, he fell in beside her.

Owena and Jinny followed, moving from bush to bush so as not to be seen.

"Yet, I am a lass," Dallis continued, "and we lasses know a thing or two about fetchin' a husband. Do you not see? 'Twas not you who chose her, but she who chose you. And why not choose such a strong and pleasin' man for a husband?"

Tavish argued, "'Tis not so, I had never seen her until that very day."

"Aye, you had not *noticed* her until that day, but she noticed you."

He drew in an exasperated breath. "What has all this to do with the MacGreagor?"

Dallis gave him her best sly grin, "Even now, you notice not who watches you from the bushes."

"I notice you often enough."

"Aye, but only if I let you. Perhaps you are bein' watched this very moment."

When he began to slow his pace, the girls were out in the open and had to quickly slip behind more bushes. Therefore, when Tavish gave the path and each bush along the way a thorough study, he saw them not. Slowly turning all the way around, he threw up his hands. "Lass, you have gone daft. No one watch..." Just then, he heard laughter, and it was much closer than he imagined. This time, it was Tavish who rolled his eyes. "Very well, I am convinced." He nodded to Dallis, and in a huff, started back toward the village.

"Do you not wish to hear the rest of it?" He did not answer. Instead, he held his head high and kept walking until he was completely out of sight. "Old grouch," she muttered.

As soon as he was gone, Jinny and Owena went to walk with her, one on each side of Dallis.

"*I* wish to hear the rest of it," said Jinny. In her hand she carried a small berry basket she made herself, just the way Dallis taught her. She had gotten so good at it, her father took the baskets to the other villages, bartered them and brought back cloths with which her mother could make new clothing. It took a while, but when each article of clothing was handed down to her, she wore each piece with pride. Being the first to wear something new was even more reason to dream of having her own home someday.

"Everyone knows Tavish fancies you, everyone knows save you," Owena scoffed. "Why do you not marry him?"

Dallis answered, "He is irksome on most days, and has no doubt passed his reluctant nature down to his sons and his grandsons, or one of them would have spoken for you, Jinny, afore now."

"And not me?" a surprised Owena asked.

Dallis sneered, "Thrice you have been asked for by a lad not an Allaway, and thrice you have refused. Now, the lads care not to persist."

"Perhaps I would not refuse if the right lad asked," said Owena.

"And who might the right lad be?" Dallis insisted.

"'Tis for me alone to know," Owena answered. Instead of falling back a little when the path got too narrow for all three of them to walk together, she pushed on until Jinny did.

Jinny simply ignored her and changed the subject. "Dallis, I find Tavish very pleasin' and more than worthy, should you change your mind about him. He may have a fault or two, but I see nothin' to fret over. He is not vile, he holds his anger, particularly where you are concerned, and his sons and grandson are the same. How could they not be?"

Dallis stopped and turned toward Jinny. "Listen well, my dear one. A lass must take special care before agreein' to marry, for an 'aye' once said cannae be unsaid."

Jinny shrugged. "All I ask is a handsome husband who is kind and gentle."

Dallis resumed walking. "'Tis what all lasses wish for, but 'tis not possible to know a lad's true nature. 'Tis why you needs let the elders choose. They hear things a lass may not hear."

"Certainly things father shall never tell us," Owena taunted. "I'll not have a MacGreagor, no matter the elders' or my father's choosin'. They are cursed."

"You believe that do you?" Dallis asked.

"Of course I do, everyone believes it. Did the MacGreagor of old not walk naked into the loch, and thereby poison the water? Father says 'twas a fortnight complete before the water smelled sweet enough to drink, and many an animal died because of it."

Once more, Dallis stopped only this time she stared at Owena. "'Twas a wretched drought that year, and 'twas the lack of water that killed the animals."

"Where did you hear that?" Jinny asked.

"From Tavish."

"Then the MacGreagor dinna bear the red mark of lightning on his chest?" Owena insisted with her hands on her hips and her eyes narrowed.

"So Tavish said," Dallis answered, "but others have a mark when they are born and they are not cursed."

An astonished Owena asked, "Aye, but you forget the tree. We have seen it for ourselves, and 'tis enough for *me* to believe the curse."

Dallis wrinkled her brow. "If the clans of old believed it, then why did they not kill the MacGreagors long ago? They dinna because there be no cause. The MacGreagors are peaceful."

"Perhaps they are too daft to attack," Owena suggested.

When Jinny stopped to pick raspberries that looked ripe enough, the others stopped too. "Kam is not daft."

"He is if he saved you from a wild cat," Owena snidely said.

Jinny glanced at the disapproving expression on Dallis' face and giggled, "True. I hear some lads love their battles more than they love their wives."

"Where did you hear that?" Owena asked.

"I heard it from a MacKellar hunter who came to barter last year," Jinny answered. "You might have heard it too, had you not been lavishin' in Reade's attention. Why you allow him to think you shall be his wife someday is a wonderment to me."

"Reade knows I am forbidden to marry an Allaway. 'Tis just a harmless pleasure."

"Harmless for you perhaps, but there is talk and some find your pleasure, as you call it, brazen."

Owena plopped two raspberries in her mouth instead of putting them in the basket. She ate them and then spitefully lifted her chin. "You mock me because Reade dinna prefer you."

"I dinna prefer Reade," Jinny shot back. "He is a weaklin' who works hard at not workin' at all. Nay, if 'twas only Reade to marry, I shan't wish to marry at all."

Dallis headed back to the village and quickened her pace at that. "Come, lasses, we best see to supper."

Jinny picked a few more berries and then hurried after them. Dallis had given her a lot to think about. Apparently, attracting the husband she wanted was harder than she suspected. A great deal of thought and circumstance went into the planning, and she'd thought of none of that before. She needed a place filled with flowers, her hair down, and...just now she could not remember what else. Oh yes, she needed to be alone. That might take some doing since she was rarely alone.

Indeed, Jinny Allaway, the second daughter of Laird Allaway, certainly had something very important to think about.

GLENDON COULD NOT HAVE wished for a nicer day, although he slept little the night before. After spending his entire life in two bedchambers filled with parents and siblings, he found the quiet of his own cottage deafening. Besides, he had a lot on his mind. Was he truly ready to take a wife, or had beating his brother out of Owena been the ultimate challenge? He thought, and more than once, of changing his mind and waiting another year or so before he married. Each time, it was a fleeting thought, for he truly did find Owena the most handsome lass he had ever seen, and he doubted there would be another like her. Equally as distressful, would be to stand aside and let Kam have her. That truly would not do. Furthermore, after all Glendon had said and done, it was now a matter of being the honorable man his father expected him to be.

With two clans currently at war, Ronson said he preferred that his sons not be unprotected, so he asked William and Birk to see to guarding them. Therefore, all was set and Glendon was about to mount his horse, when Kam rode up and joined the other three. "Ready, brother?"

"You have not changed your mind and wish to stay home?"

"Nay. What kind of brother would I be if I let you go alone at a time like this?"

Glendon stared at his brother for a moment, dropped his gaze, and got on his horse. "Very well, but when we arrive, you shall not hinder me."

"I have no idea of hinderin' you," said Kam as he followed his brother to the main road, and together they turned toward the Allaway village.

"You dinna wear the sword," Glendon mentioned to his brother.

"Nay. The tip is broken off, and Father said 'twould not protect me well enough for travel."

"I see."

The four of them rode in silence for a time, with William in front, the brothers side-by-side, and Birk in back, before Kam said, "'Tis early. Perhaps we might go for a swim first."

Glendon chuckled. "So you may drown me?"

"I thought of it, but Father would nary believe 'twas an accident."

"You be not as daft as I thought."

"Brother, you thought me daft?" Kam sarcastically asked. "'Tis only right, for I believe you daft as well. Yet, you could use a good scrubbin'."

"Am I not wearin' clean clothin'? Aye, I am. I bathed yesterday, and so did you."

"Did I? I had forgotten that." Behind him, Birk snickered, but neither Kam nor Glendon seemed to notice.

"You forget little, and you know it," Glendon said. "What be the real reason you wish to stop?"

"There is somethin' I wish to say to you before you marry."

Glendon finally halted his horse, folded one arm, rested the elbow of his other arm on his hand, and then laid his left hand against the side of his face. "Have you thought of a way to take Owena for yourself?"

Kam scoffed. "Nay, for I have decided you may have her. I shall be far more pleased with her sister."

"Why do I not believe you?"

"'Tis true. I do not fancy Owena as much as I once did, and Father is right. I know not what she is about."

"Nor do I, and I am not persuaded otherwise."

"You are not persuaded otherwise because you do not think clearly."

Glendon rolled his eyes. "And you do?"

"Of course, if you do not truly desire Owena, I shall agree to let you have her sister."

With his back legs, Glendon's horse took several side steps forcing Glendon to face his brother instead of being beside him. "Halt, Oranite," Glendon commanded. His horse immediately obeyed. "'Tis twice you have said of her sister. Is there somethin' you wish to tell me?"

"What could I possibly have to tell you?"

"For one, do you recall her name?"

"Of course I do, she is Jinny. Jinny shall suit me very well for she is upright."

"William," Glendon said, "you were with my brother when he went to the Allaway village last. Did you find Jinny upright?"

"Aye, Jinny tried to convince her father to let us have the skin of the wildcat in return for savin' her."

"That *was* upright of her," Glendon had to agree. "And Owena? Is she not upright?"

"I know not...for she spoke little."

Glendon noticed when William did not readily answer. "Ah, then there is somethin' my brother does not say of Jinny. Out with it William."

William turned his horse around, looked first at Kam and then at Glendon. "Owena said she wished not to be separated from her sister, and shall not marry unless Jinny is also wed to a MacGreagor."

"I see."

Relieved to be out of the conversation, William turned his horse back around so he could watch for danger instead.

Glendon once more turned to his brother. "Then your problem is twofold. One, you must convince Owena to reject my advances, and then you must convince me to marry her sister." When William started down the road again, Glendon got his horse moving as well. "I cannae wait to see what becomes of us both." Had he looked behind him, he would have seen Kam's frustrated frown.

Witness to it all but keeping silent, Birk was about to closely follow when he noticed the nay of a horse not far behind him. "Wait," he said to the others, halted his horse and turned it completely around. "Who goes there?" he commanded. A moment passed, and then another before Cerdic guided his horse onto the road and exposed himself.

"Have you permission to follow?" Kam asked.

"Not precisely," Cerdic answered.

"He means nay," said Glendon.

"Be gone with you," said Kam.

Cerdic promised, "Kam, soon I shall have to choose a wife...well, perhaps not that soon, but I wish to know how 'tis done. I shall not be in the way."

"I say let him come," said Glendon. "I care not to take him back, and 'tis not safe for him alone."

"Very well," Kam said, "but see that you stay well away from us when we reach the village, or I shall have a harsh word with your father when we return."

Glendon chuckled, "I suspect his father already wishes to have a harsh word with him." His comment made the others chuckle, and when William got them started down the road once more, Birk motioned for the boy to get in front of him. Therefore, the four MacGreagors became five.

CHAPTER 7

NOT ONLY DID THE MACGREAGORS know the brothers were headed for the Allaway village, an Allaway hunter spotted them coming and swiftly rode ahead to alert his clan.

Jinny was outside working in the garden when she heard that not one, but five MacGreagor lads were coming. The day long awaited had finally come and for a moment, she was awestruck. Then it occurred to her that Kam might not be coming to make her his wife. For all she knew, the MacGreagors would ride past her village and go off to barter with the MacKellar, or even the Battie.

Just in case, she dropped her wooden shovel, and hurried home to change clothes and brush her hair. That very morning, she decided she might better compete against her sister if she wore her waist-length hair unbound. Her heart was all a flutter, and her hands were unsteady as she rushed through the door and then disappeared into one of the separated rooms, the one she shared with her sister. She paid no attention to her mother when she came to the doorway and stood gawking while Jinny changed clothes. At last, she was dressed in a green skirt that had but a few small patches, and quickly buttoned her soft leather vest.

She remembered to breathe, pulled the string out of her hair, quickly unbraided it and grabbed the bristle brush off the shelf. When she was finished and as satisfied as possible with her appearance, she gave her mother a hug and then reemerged into the great room.

Sitting beside the warm fire, Owena did nothing to improve her looks, Jinny noticed, which was just fine with her. Then again, she had never seen a day when Owena did not look pleasing. She tried not to sigh, and instead thought about where she should be when Kam came – inside or outside? She decided on outside, went back to the garden and picked up her shovel.

If the others noticed the change in her, none of them mentioned it.

As was usual in the mornings, the Allaway women were busy hauling water, and keeping the children out of trouble as well as out of danger, while the men tended the livestock and hauled more dry wood with which to build the evening fire. Chickens squawked, the dogs barked, and the elders looked exhausted even at that time of day. At least the courtyard, such as it was, was clean enough to be presentable.

A second awful feeling washed over her. What if Kam was not among the MacGreagors? What if he changed his mind and decided against an Allaway bride? Although she tried not to watch the path, she could not help herself. If only someone would come to give her more information. Had they turned down the path to her village or not? Was Kam with them, or not? No one knew, and when she saw Dallis watching her, she bowed her head and pretended to dig a slight trench in a garden row.

It was not until one of the Allaway men said something about visitors, that she dared raise her gaze. William, one of the men who had come to rescue her, was the first to appear, followed by one she did not know, and then...to her relief, came Kam. She smiled and completely forgot all about pretending to be working in the garden. Instead, she kept her eyes glued on Kam hoping he would see her, and at least return her smile. He did not. In fact, he looked a little perplexed.

The MacGreagors nodded to the Allaway men, dismounted at the edge of the forest, and then tied their horses. At last, they walked into the courtyard, where the four men stood in a row with a boy taking up a position behind Kam.

Laird Allaway, himself having helped haul wood for the evening fire, paused in his work and went to greet Kam. "So, you've come back?"

"Aye. This be my brother Glendon, our guards, William and Birk, and the boy...he paused and looked back to see where Cerdic was. "The laddie be Cerdic.

"You have come to choose a wife?" Laird Allaway persisted.

Kam nodded. "Aye."

"And you?" Laird Allaway asked Glendon. "Shall you marry the one he dinna choose?"

Glendon raised an eyebrow, but he said nothing in the way of contradicting his brother in front of the Allaway. "Perhaps." His answer seemed to abundantly please the clan's laird. He looked around, but the one called Owena was nowhere in sight. Glendon noticed several of the women watching him, some older, some younger, and could not tell which might be Owena's sister, Jinny. "Our father has forbid us to marry until we have learned the ways of your daughters."

"Learned their ways?" Laird Allaway asked. "Their ways are the same as any lasses' ways."

Glendon glanced around a second time, and then shifted his weight to the other foot. "Have you not two daughters?"

"Aye," Laird Allaway admitted. "Jinny be in the garden, and Owena be in the cottage. Shall I send for her?"

"No need, Father," Owena said as she opened the door and came out. Her hair was down too, her smile was warm, and when she walked, her hips swayed as if to some unheard music.

It was then Jinny's heart sank, for Kam's smile was for Owena, and thus far he had not even looked at her. She returned Glendon's nod, but it was clear that Kam's brother's smile was for Owena too. All was lost, and since there was no need to impress Kam, she laid the shovel back down and tightly folded her arms. Then again, there was still a scant touch of hope, for the MacGreagor insisted on knowing Owena's ways before Kam agreed to the marriage. It was indeed only a scant hope, but it *was* something. Surely a time, or a time and a half with Owena, would betray her true nature. Jinny noticed the lad slip out from behind Kam, and come around to the side of William, she supposed, to hear better what was being said. Oddly, the lad kept a closer eye on Kam's brother than on Kam. Perhaps all was not as it seemed. But then, all lads his age were prone to make more of a situation than was necessary.

Laird Allaway glanced at his eldest daughter, turned his back to her, and then half smiled at Jinny. "Well, what say you, MacGreagor? Ask, and I shall tell you of their ways and save you the trouble of takin' the time to learn them."

"And what then do we tell our father?" Glendon insisted.

Laird Allaway considered that for a moment, "Truly, your father has exceedingly strange ways."

"That he does," Kam sarcastically said, giving his brother an annoyed glance.

"What do you suggest then?" the laird asked.

Glendon ignored Kam. "Well," he answered, "Perhaps we might take them for a walk."

"We?"

"Aye, my brother and I."

Laird Allaway nodded first to William and then to Birk. "And the others shall walk as well?"

Kam quickly took over the conversation. "Father insists on our protection. We hear the Lennox are preparin' for battle."

Allaway stood up a little straighter. "Whom do they think to attack?"

"Likely, the MacKellar."

The older man looked greatly relieved. "Aye, the MacKellar and not us. Very good indeed."

"The walk?" Kam reminded him.

"Aye, very well, you may walk with them, but mind you, I shall know if anythin' is amiss when you bring them back."

Kam nodded first at her father and then at Owena.

"Come Jinny," Owena said.

That was not how Jinny dreamed it would be. She hoped to be alone with Kam, looking very pleasing, and surrounded by flowers just as Tavish's wife had been. She had it all planned. Jinny would slip away from the others to a particular place on the flower laden hillside and wait for Kam to come looking for her. They would talk, he would profess his love for her, and...

"Dearest Jinny," Owena was pleasantly asking. "Do you not wish to come with us?"

Dearest? Owena never called her dearest before. So that's how it was to be. Owena's lies were exposed, she wanted Kam after all, and she was determined to charm her way into his arms. Jinny took a deep breath and forced her feet to move. "Comin'." She had no nod nor smile for any of them, even when the men allowed she and her sister to walk ahead of them. Worse still, Owena was leading them down the forest-lined path to the very hillside Jinny had picked out earlier – the one filled with spring flowers. That Owena looked back twice to smile at Kam did not go unnoticed by Jinny, and she felt each step she took brought her closer to certain doom.

At length, Owena stopped and turned around. When Kam came closer before he stopped, she laid a finger on his chest and then looked up into his eyes. "You may ask your questions now."

Kam grinned and took hold of her hand. "I cannae think of one just now."

"I can," Glendon said. "Is it true you and your sister wish to marry into the same clan?"

Kam gave his brother an annoyed glance while Owena quickly nodded.

Jinny said nothing and instead stared at the ground. Nay, she wanted to say, but did not. Her legs suddenly felt heavy, her head was awash with muddle, and she might have screamed had she gotten enough of her wits about her to do it. Suddenly, Glendon had ahold of her arm to steady her.

"Are you unwell?" he asked.

Embarrassed, she half smiled. "I am quite well, thank you." He seemed reluctant to let go, and fortunately held on long enough to let her settle her emotions. She was at war with her sister and she should at least fight back. Yet, what would Kam think of her if she made a spectacle of herself? No, she should wait until Kam made his intentions perfectly clear, and then she would throttle her sister!

"Perhaps we should sit down," Kam offered. He helped Owena sit in the tall grass, sat next to her, waited until she spread her skirt just so, and then reached for her hand again. It not only made Owena smile, she did not pull her hand away, as a more respectable young woman might have while in the company of others.

With no other choice, Glendon took Jinny's hand, helped her sit, and then moved a decent distance away before he sat down. Cerdic was nowhere in sight, and the MacGreagor guards hung back to allow the young couples some measure of privacy.

"We watched you," Jinny finally found the courage to say, though she did not direct her remark specifically to either man.

"Watched us?" Kam asked. "When?"

"Yesterday," Jinny answered. "We happened to go to the Lennox village and wanted to see the lightnin' tree."

"Aye," said Kam, "the lightnin' tree."

"Who be the elder standin' atop the hill?" Owena asked.

"'Twas likely our father," Glendon answered.

"And the mule?" Owena wanted to know. "Be it a MacGreagor or a Lennox mule?"

"A MacGreagor, sadly," Glendon answered. "We think to give Calla away, but..."

"Give it away?" a surprised Jinny asked. "Why?"

"Because," Kam answered, "Calla dinna work, nor stay out of the garden less we tie her up."

Jinny started to say, "Is there no way..."

"Why are the MacGreagor lasses so happy?" Owena interrupted. "They sing while they work."

"Are Allaway lasses not happy?" a concerned Glendon asked.

"They sing because 'tis spring," Kam answered.

"I am always happy in spring too," Owena said, her eyes fluttering as she fixed them on Kam's. The expression on Kam's face betrayed his feelings as well. Obviously, he thought Owena irresistible.

Jinny thought their flirtatious display nauseating. For her, there was no further doubting what the outcome of this day would be, and once more, Jinny felt the urge to scream. Owena was never happy, be it spring, autumn, summer, or winter. Jinny might have allowed herself to scream, had it not been for her most fervent secondary desire – if Owena married Kam, Jinny would finally be shed of her sister.

Curious, she tried to read the expression on Glendon's face, but he was looking down, seemingly choosing a blade of grass to pull and toy with. Was Kam's brother uninterested, or just as disgusted as Jinny? Hopefully, he was not contemplating marrying her for the sake of his brother's unrestrained desires. About that, she was not truly worried, for what man would do such a thing, even for the love of a brother? She knew of no Allaway man who would. Even so, she decided to pay far more attention to the expressions on Glendon's face than on Kam's.

"Brother," said Kam as he let go of Owena's hand and got to his feet, "I wish a word with you."

"I suspected you might," Glendon answered. He took hold of Kam's hand, and let his brother pull him up. He nodded first to Owena, and then to Jinny, before he followed Kam into the nearby trees.

WITH GLENDON FOLLOWING, Kam walked far enough into the forest to still see the sisters and the guards, but to be certain none could hear him. Then he stopped, turned to his brother and put a hand on Glendon's shoulder. "Surely you can see Owena prefers me to you," Kam said.

"I am not convinced."

"Brother, do you not see I must have her?"

"Of that I have no doubt, but Owena knows not she has a choice. Therefore, how can she be certain of her desire?"

"She sees only me and not you. Can I be mistaken on that accord? Nay, I think not."

"And if you are right, you wish me to marry Jinny?"

"Brother, 'tis hard pressed to say which of us has gone daft, but I would surely think to do it for *your* sake."

When Glendon started to walk away, Kam grabbed his arm. "Very well then, to have her, I shall give over the MacGreagor sword."

Stunned, Glendon slowly turned back and let his mouth fall open. "You would give up your birthright, your place as Laird of the clan, for a lass?"

Kam's answer was quick and stern. "I would."

"You care not what Father shall say?"

"Father need not know. I shall tell the clan after Father has passed."

Glendon smirked. "Unless you can think of a way to deny you said it."

Kam glanced at William and Birk. "Will two witnesses not satisfy?"

"Wait, allow me a moment to think." Glendon walked a few feet away, turned his back and covered his face with his hands. Deep down inside he felt he would be a much better laird than his brother, but what would the clan think of it? Would they be disappointed, would they honor and follow him, the younger of the two brothers? His first inclination was yes, but was he certain? No, he could not be certain.

And then there was the question of Owena. Perhaps his attachment to her was not as strong as he pretended, and therefore he suspected that, if given sufficient time, she would not be that hard to get over.

If he agreed, heretofore he would be married to Jinny. Kam lied. She looked nothing at all like her sister. Jinny was perhaps pleasing enough in her appearance, but there was one thing that gave him great pause – Jinny seemed the downhearted sort. Was she that way always, or just on this occasion? If the answer was always, what would his mother think of her? What would the clan think, and what would his life truly be like? He could not know. There were far too many questions, and he had no clear answers.

Yet, he truly believed he would make a better laird than his brother, and would not any other man, no matter the cost, marry wrongly for the sake of the clan? His father would, of that much he was certain. Glendon finally took his hands off his face, and turned around. "You are willin' to pledge it in front of William and Birk?"

Kam answered, "Aye, and anyone else you so desire."

"No one else must know for fear Father hear it. It would break his heart."

Kam slowly turned his determined expression into a smile. "Agreed."

Glendon still was not sure he should trust his brother. "Give me your word. Father is to hear that Owena denied me and chose you, and nothin' more."

"'Tis true. She does prefer me and not you."

"You shall not regret this. When that day comes, I shall pledge to honor and follow you as my laird."

Glendon hoped that day would not come anytime soon. It meant the death of Ronson, and he loved and admired his father. At length, he motioned for William and Birk to join them.

Unable to hide his joy, Kam explained the situation, and repeated his pledge to give the sword to Glendon. William and Birk exchanged worried glances, but finally nodded. Kam touched both guards on the shoulder and then hurried back to ask for Owena.

From the edge of the forest, Glendon, William and Birk watched as Kam helped both of the girls get up. They could not hear what was said, but the happy expression on Owena's face, while the downhearted look on Jinny's, left nothing to the imagination. Glendon took a deep breath, and then went to join his brother.

Owena appeared to be bursting with joy at first, but then she narrowed her eyes at Kam. "As I said, I shall not marry you unless Jinny marries a MacGreagor as well. I simply cannae live without her." She looked directly at Glendon and waited for him to say something.

Jinny's plea was unspoken, but there nonetheless. Please say you will not marry me.

Instead, Glendon said, "I dinna prefer her, but…"

Jinny's expression instantly changed from disappointment to downright hostility. She put her hands on her hips and glared at Glendon, "Then we are even, for I dinna prefer you either!" She turned right around and marched down the path toward the village.

"But you must marry him!" Owena persisted. "I cannae marry if…"

"Then you shall not marry!" Jinny shouted.

"Sister wait!" Owena loudly said as she started after her. "Sister?"

Jinny stopped, slumped, and did not bother to turn around. "What?" Any other day, Owena would have been howling with anger by now. Not this day. This day she was trying to impress a prospective husband, and Jinny was not fooled by her sister's shallowness for one single moment. She thought to completely shatter Owena's false character, and she knew just how to do it too, but what then? Would Kam decide against her after all, and choose Jinny instead? Even if he did, Jinny had seen enough to give second, third and fourth thought to any proposal Kam might have.

With her back to the MacGreagors, Owena lowered her voice and began to pout. "You dinna love me, you never did."

"I do love you, but not enough to marry against my will."

"Lasses marry against their will all the time. Glendon shall make a good husband."

"And you know this havin' only just met him?"

"He is quiet, the same as you and he is not unsightly. You said yourself you'd not mind an unsightly lad..."

Jinny finally turned around to face her sister. "...if he loved me. Clearly, he dinna even fancy me in the least. Therefore, I shall not have him!"

Abruptly, Owena leaned forward, put her head next to her sister's ear and whispered her threat.

Jinny's mouth dropped. "I was only six and you told me to do it!"

Owena pulled back, and this time she gritted her teeth. "I shall have Kam and you shall go with me, no matter what I must say or do to have my way." She walked past Jinny and quickly continued on down the path.

Jinny glanced at the four MacGreagors watching her, threw up her hands, turned around and followed her sister to the village. She knew exactly what Owena would do – she would beg their father until he demanded Jinny marry, but Jinny was not worried. Owena's spurts of loud sobbing and then fits of anger had worked well enough in the past, but it would not work this time! Besides, Owena would not display her true nature until she was certain she had lost Kam for good.

As it turned out, instead of going to beg her father, Owena went to stand with her mother and several other women. It was obvious Owena let them know what was at hand, for all of them turned to stare at Jinny.

Still furious, Jinny went back to the garden, picked up the shovel, and resumed her work. A few moments later, her father came to talk to her. When she ignored him, he took the shovel away. "Well?"

When she looked up at him, she answered, "Owena is betrothed. I am not!"

"But you must be. Daughter, be reasonable," said Laird Allaway. "Is it not plain that Owena needs be married off? She tempts the lads, and 'tis only a matter of time until she shames us all."

Jinny hung her head. No one loved a father more than she loved hers, and disappointing him would hurt her deeply. Still, there had to be a way to talk him out of it. "I know, Father, you have said it all before."

"And your mother? She insists the two of you be nearby where she can see to your health. The MacGreagors are not healthy, as you well know."

"They look healthy to me," she argued.

"Aye, but looks are deceivin'."

"You would not wish me to become unhealthy too. Life with them would surely..."

"Jinny, your sister..."

"Father, what about me? Why must I sacrifice my happiness for her benefit? Let her make her own happiness and leave me to mine."

Laird Allaway narrowed his eyes. "Dinna force me to command it of you."

She glanced to one side and then the other, "What about the curse? What shall the Allaways say if both of your daughters become cursed as well?"

He took a deep frustrated breath. "I see no evidence of a curse. Nay, daughter, you shall marry and you shall do it this very day! I must have relief from your sister's foolishness, or I shall surely die sooner than I should. You know I am right. A husband for Owena is the only remedy for her unthinkable ways. Jinny, I beg of you, do it for my sake." With that, Laird Allaway handed the shovel back and walked away.

There it was – the ultimate persuasion. If she agreed, she would be miserable, and if she did not agree and her father died, she would live a life of guilt and remorse. When she looked, Kam, Glendon, William, and Birk had arrived and all four were watching her. She was about to cry, but she held back, for she would not succumb to putting on a public display. On the other side of the fire pit, her mother stood beside Owena and at least half the clan was watching her too. She should, and eventually would nod her consent, but not just yet.

Was there nothing more to be said – no way to avoid a fate worse than death?

Nay, she supposed, there was no way. At long last, she nodded, but not to Glendon, not to Kam, not to Owena, but to her mother. Instantly, Owena shrieked with delight and began to run to her. Owena's hug was fierce, nearly knocked her over, and there was nothing Jinny hated more than the look of delight on her sister's face.

Once more Owena had gotten her way.

WHOM OWENA CHOSE TO marry was of no real concern to young Cerdic. While Owena was bonnie, he supposed, he saw nothing extraordinary about the other one. Not only that, he had been so busy making the acquaintance of the Allaway, he neglected to spy on Kam and Glendon so he could see just how choosing a bride was done.

Standing with several of the men who were busy building their evening fire, he thought to delight them with a MacGreagor story he doubted any of them had ever heard before. At first, he did not speak loudly for fear the other MacGreagors were listening. Owena and her sister had gone inside their cottage to gather their things, or so Cerdic supposed, which meant Kam and Glendon might hear him. He glanced around, lowered his voice, and began his story.

"A Giant," one of the astonished Allaway men nearly shouted. "I believe it not. 'Tis but a tall tale."

"Nay, 'tis true!" Cerdic swore. When he looked back, the other MacGreagors were now watching too, and Glendon was even smiling, so he felt no need to continue in a lowered tone of voice. "The MacGreagor giant measured 40 hands, at least." This time he had everyone's attention, and most laughed. Cerdic frowned. "Believe me not, if you wish, but 'tis true, right enough."

"Well then," said another, "what became of him?"

"He died, I suppose. 'Twas long before I was born. At the time, the MacGreagors lived in the far north, and..."

"And you say your giant frightened a hundred Vikings away?"

"Perhaps not a hundred, but..." Cerdic's words were interrupted by still more laughter, a few taunting shouts, and the rolling of eyes. He looked around then, hoping Kam would back up his story, only to discover both Kam and Glendon standing right behind him. "Tell them, Kam. Say 'tis not a tall tale." To Cerdic's horror, Kam gave the others a disgusted glance, shook his head and walked away.

Glendon had his arms folded. "Do I not hear your father callin' you?"

Cerdic's eyes widened, "Truly?"

"Best be gettin'..." Glendon dinna have time to finish his sentence before Cerdic ran to his horse, untied the reins, and swung up on. Horrified, he raced the horse up the path toward the road. Behind him, the Allaway were still laughing, but he did not care. He had more important things to worry about, especially if his father truly had left the sheep to come looking for him.

CHAPTER 8

IT TOOK TIME FOR JINNY to collect and put her things in a sack – perhaps quite a lot longer than it would have, had she been happy to be leaving. The sickeningly excited Owena chatted away and cared to brush her hair again. When her mother presented her with a flower ringlet to wear on her head, her smile actually seemed genuine. "'Tis most handsome, Mother. I thank you."

However, the one Mistress Allaway gave to Jinny had twice the flowers. Jinny hugged her mother, and although she hadn't bothered to brush her hair again, she allowed her mother to put it on her head. Jinny pondered, if only for a moment, if her mother did so trying to make Jinny look just as pleasing as her sister. It was of no use, for her future husband had already spoken his lack of desire for her, and nothing, not even an abundance of flowers in her hair, could take his words from her mind.

There remained one hope still for Jinny, although a faint one. If Owena and Kam married first and she then declined to agree, it would be too late. Owena would already be married. With that in mind when Owena and her mother went outside, Jinny decided to buy time by brushing her hair again after all. She carefully listened and when everyone outside got quiet, she held her breath. Marriages were elaborate affairs for kings, but in the clans little more had to be said than a simple declaration of the couple's desire to be united. A word, a nod, a cheer of the clan and...

"Jinny? Are you not comin'?" Owena said, yanking the cottage door open.

All hope was finally lost.

In a cloud of mental fatigue, she set the brush aside, left the flower wreath on the table, walked out the door and gave her consent to be married to Glendon MacGreagor. It was done then, and there was no undoing it. She cared not to listen to her sister's part in the simple ceremony, tried her best not to hate Kam for choosing wrongly, and looked not once at her husband. Even when he tied her sack on his horse, lifted her up, and then mounted behind her, did she notice his very existence. Instead, she looked at her parents as if to say goodbye forever, acknowledged each of her younger siblings with a nod, and then allowed Glendon to take her away.

As tired as she was, she held herself upright, vowing not to lean against Glendon or to touch him more than was absolutely necessary. Nor did he needlessly touch her, save for the usual way of putting one arm around her to keep her from falling off. There was one thing to be grateful for – at least they were in front of the giggling Owena and therefore Jinny was not forced to watch more of her sister's disgraceful display. After all, she had seen it all before.

Once more, William was in the lead and when they were not yet halfway home, William held up his hand to stop and to silence them. Of course, Owena could not be silenced, even when the others feared danger. Jinny felt Glendon turn to look back at his brother, who somehow managed to get Owena to stop talking. It was then they heard the pounding of many horse's hooves coming up the road. At William's direction, the small group darted off the road and went deep into the woods. Even then, Owena was more interested in her own delights than in being quiet, and when Jinny finally decided to glare at her silly sister, Kam had found a way to quiet her. He kissed Owena and did not stop.

The sounds of men on horses increased, passed by, and then steadily decreased until they could be heard no more.

"MacKellar," Birk whispered to the others.

"Aye," said Glendon.

"I must warn the Lennox," said Birk.

Glendon glanced at his brother, saw that he paid no attention to anything but the woman in his arms, and nodded. Instantly, Birk guided his horse through the woods, taking a little known short cut.

"They fight?" Jinny whispered.

"Aye," Glendon answered. "'Tis been soon comin'."

"Why do they fight?"

"Two hunters, one a MacKellar and the other a Lennox each shot the same red deer," he explained, keeping his voice low. "'Tis over it that they argue."

She slightly turned her head his direction. "Why did they not cut the deer in half?"

"They did, but the MacKellar accuses the Lennox of takin' the larger half. The Lennox," Glendon continued, "vowed to share the next red deer with the MacKellar, but he dinna."

"When was this? I have heard nothin' of it."

"These three years."

Jinny covered her mouth to muffle her laughter. Then a sudden thought crossed her mind and made her next question far more serious. "Shall the MacGreagors also fight?"

"Nay, we dinna fight unless attacked." Glendon nodded to William, tightened his arm around his bride, and urged his horse to follow William back to the road.

It was odd. The Allaway men rarely explained such things to the Allaway women, yet she'd been married to Glendon less than half a day, and already he took the trouble of explaining what was happening to her. It was very odd indeed.

Owena giggled, and when she did, Jinny heard Kam tell her to be quiet. Jinny rolled her eyes. She simply could not wait to see how well that was going to turn out, yet in this case it was important for her sister to obey. With Birk gone, they had no one to guard them from behind and Kam needed to be alert. It mattered not to Owena, who again giggled and made an unfamiliar purring sound. Horrified and disgusted, Jinny bowed her head and closed her eyes.

To Jinny's relief, William got them moving faster, which made it impossible for Owena to do anything but hang on.

BEHIND THEM, IAN BATTIE tried to keep up without being seen. He had only just arrived when Kam MacGreagor put his beloved Owena on a horse and rode away with her. Before then, Ian feared what the Lennox told him was untrue – Kam was not to marry her. Now, it looks as though he had. Just to make certain, Ian continued to follow. He too heard the MacKellar coming, and slipped into the forest just in time.

After the MacKellar and the MacGreagors were gone, he eased his horse back onto the road and took a moment to assess the situation. From the way Owena was hanging all over Kam, it was plain to see, they were in love. That made it so much the better, for Kam and therefore the rest of the MacGreagors would suffer great pain, and be more than willing to trade Owena for Teva when the time came. As well, such as that would certainly serve Ronson MacGreagor right for not giving Teva to him when he asked.

He turned his horse around and headed home. Now that his plan was coming together and his hope was renewed, he could easily imagine how it would be on his wedding day. Of course, his Teva would never put on such a public display as Owena, that much he was certain of.

The sun would be down soon, the moonless night promised total darkness, and the road might still be filled with angry and upset MacKellars, but he felt happier than he had in weeks. He galloped his horse down the road as fast as it would go, all the while with a grin on his face.

BY THE TIME THEY RODE into the nearly deserted village, the MacGreagor men were on the other side of the hill. They were armed and ready to fight should the battle spill over onto their side, and paid little attention to the return of their Laird's sons. Atop the hill stood Ronson facing the border with the Lennox. Himself armed, save for a glance their direction, he studied the situation, and made ready to alert his men should any Lennox or MacKellar come running.

Glendon quickly dismounted, pulled Jinny down, left her beside his horse, and then ran to stand beside his father. Kam, on the other hand, took the time to proudly present Owena to his mother.

"You married Owena?" his surprised mother asked.

"I shall explain it later," Kam whispered.

"Explain what?" Owena wanted to know.

Mayzie motioned for Jinny to come too, ushered them both inside the laird's house, and then closed the door. On the floor sat Ronson's two younger children, obediently waiting for word that the danger was over.

"Sit," Mayzie said, motioning toward the table. She bolted the door and then sat down opposite the brides.

"I hear no fightin'," Jinny said.

"Nay, nor do we. Perhaps they have found a way of resolvin' it..." Mayzie started to say.

"Two Allaway fought last spring," Owena interrupted. "We lost a very good lad before it ended."

Jinny ignored her sister's nonsensical ramblings and instead stared at the wood floor. She remembered that day well. Owena agreed to marry an Allaway and then changed her mind. When the man drew his sword and was set to strike Owena, two more Allaway drew theirs as well. In the end, the man who laid claim to Owena was dead. It was a very sad day and Laird Allaway would not let Owena attend the burial, for fear the clan would turn on his eldest daughter. In time, most of the clan set aside their resentment, but there were those who vowed to openly revolt, should Owena again be betrothed to an Allaway. In that regard, Laird Allaway was right – both he and the clan were better off without Owena.

Jinny took another of the several upset deep breaths she had taken already that day. Owena was now a MacGreagor, and unfortunately, so was Jinny.

Before Owena could finish another story that was less than half true, Ronson came to the door and shouted, "'Tis safe now!"

Relieved, Mayzie got up and quickly lifted the door bolt. She greeted her husband with a warm hug, and then introduced Kam's wife to him.

Just as surprised as Mayzie, Ronson also asked, "You have married Kam?"

Owena was perplexed. "Did you not give him permission to marry?"

"Aye," Ronson said. "I was..." he stopped in midsentence when he took the time to notice Jinny. "And you are?"

"She is my sister," Owena answered. "She is lately married to Glendon."

Both of Ronson's eyebrows shot up, and he was hard pressed to hide his disturbed expression. The MacGreagor laird turned right around and went out the door. "KAM!" he shouted.

Mayzie followed her husband, Owena rushed out behind her and went looking for Kam, and the children breezed past Jinny to watch the excitement. Jinny simply paused in the doorway to watch. By then, Birk had come back from warning the Lennox, and the men were beginning to disarm. The women had come out of the cottages and everyone was gathering in the courtyard.

"What happened?" Rossalyn asked her husband.

Birk gave his wife a quick hug. "The Lennox offered a calf as payment, the MacKellar accepted and went home."

"Thank goodness," Rossalyn sighed.

"KAM!" Ronson bellowed again.

His eldest son's grin quickly faded when he turned around to face his father.

"How is it your brother has not the wife he intended?"

Owena took hold of Kam's arm. "What does he mean?"

Jinny finally let the door to the Laird's house close, and moved so she could see Kam better. Something was amiss, but she did not know what.

"Father, 'twas meant to be," Kam said. He shed himself of Owena's grasp and then went to stand directly in front of Ronson. Not far away, Glendon clasped his hands behind his back and stayed where he was.

"How is it *you* married Owena and not your brother? Did I not give him first choice?"

Kam lowered his voice. "Owena dinna prefer Glendon, she preferred me. Is that not so, brother?"

As he agreed to do, Glendon nodded.

Ronson then turned his attention to Glendon. "And you have also taken a wife, a different wife?"

Glendon did not look away when he answered, "Aye, Father."

"Her name is Jinny," Kam tried to explain, "and she is..."

Ronson was having none of Kam's explanations. "I shall judge for myself what your brother's wife is."

"Aye, Father," Kam said.

"Is there somethin' more I should know," Ronson asked his eldest son, "for 'tis not what I expected."

"Nay, father," Kam assured him, "Owena..."

Glendon interrupted, "Owena would not marry him unless I wed her sister."

"I see. And you did so just to please your brother?" an incredulous Ronson asked, "the same brother you constantly battle with over the least little..."

"We have grown up, Father," Kam tried.

"Grown up, have you? Aye, you best be grown up now that you have wives." When he looked at William as if to ask a question, William quickly walked away. Ronson pondered the situation for a moment, and then said, "Well, if that be the case, we must celebrate." He was not smiling, but several in the clan were.

Suddenly, Owena was standing next to Jinny, had leaned closer and said, "So Glendon wished to marry me. How happy I am that he married you instead. I dinna favor Glendon."

This time, Jinny did not bother to hide her fury, "Nor did I!" She wanted to cry, she wanted to scream, and she wanted to be alone for once – but that was not to be.

FROM HIS VANTAGE POINT tending the sheep on a hillside, poor Cerdic saw the brothers, their guards, and the Allaway sisters arrive. He left the Allaway village before the marriages took place and all the way home he wondered which married which. He too was surprised when the bonnie lass arrived on Kam's horse. He suspected an uproar and by the look on some faces, he was right, yet there he was – stuck too far away to hear. Cerdic desperately wanted to, he even decided to leave his post and run home, but when he looked, his father was shaking his head.

Thoroughly disappointed, Cerdic turned his back to the village and headed off to look for more lost sheep.

WHILE KAM AND GLENDON were being congratulated by the men and some of the women, their mother went to talk to her new daughters-in-law. As was the way of most women, Mayzie absentmindedly touched her partly extended stomach. Jinny warmly smiled at her, but Owena was far more interested in watching Kam.

"Come climb the hill with me," said Mayzie, "and see the land. I am certain you shall soon love this glen as much as I do."

"Not me," Owena said. "I dinna climb hills." She turned away and when Kam smiled at her, she went to be by his side.

Mayzie hid her amazement well. "And you, Jinny, do you climb hills?"

Jinny nodded. "Many and often." She made her new mother-in-law smile, which meant, Jinny decided, that Mayzie would not be fooled by Owena for long. It was a small indication that she might find some measure of happiness among the MacGreagors after all, although it remained to be seen.

It was an easy climb and when they reached the top, Mayzie said, "My husband and I come here each morning to feel the wind and to spend what little quiet time we have together. I deeply treasure it."

"You love your husband?"

"Very much."

Jinny had to admit seeing the loch and the forest from the hilltop was breathtaking, but she had other things on her mind. "What must I do?"

"Do?" Mayzie asked.

"Aye. What shall my chores be?"

"The same as the chores all wives do for their families. Is there a particular chore you like best?"

"I like makin' baskets and other things out of heather."

"Good, we can always use more baskets. What do you like least?"

Jinny hesitated at first, but decided to say it anyway, "I dinna care to milk the cows."

Mayzie smiled, "Nor do I. Fortunately, we have enough young ones here to take that chore over. What else do you care not to do?"

"Nothin' else, just milkin'. I am in fear of gettin' stepped on."

"I find that a just fear. More than one lass has suffered a hurt foot in that very manner." When she looked, Owena had her arms wrapped around Kam and others in the clan seemed shocked by it. "Oh dear." Mayzie said no more in front of Jinny, and instead turned around so she and Jinny could look the opposite direction. "The stonewall marks the land of the Lennox."

"I know, Owena and I went to the Lennox village yesterday, and came to see the lightning tree." Was that just yesterday, Jinny wondered.

"I see. Well, I am glad you dinna turn your nose up at us. You married my son and now you have willingly come to live with us."

Jinny quickly turned her head away so Mayzie could not see the truth in her expression. She was not there willingly, and certainly not happily. It occurred to her that she could run down the hill, jump over the lowest part of the stone wall, and flee this place and all the people in it – especially Owena. Her thoughts of escape were interrupted.

"Jinny, have I misspoken?"

She quickly turned back and smiled to reassure Glendon's mother. "Nay, 'tis a place of great beauty and I am pleased to be here."

"Good. Now, I have kept you from your husband too long." She took Jinny's hand, and together they walked back down the hill.

On a table in the courtyard, the women had begun to lay out various dishes for the celebration. Most consisted of pots of mutton stew that had been cooking most of the day, loaves of bread, sweet butter, and raspberries. It was the best they could do with last year's stores nearly gone from the cellars. Soon, they would have fresh vegetables, but not quite yet. Until then, the hunters were counted on to supplement their supplies by providing more meat with which to fill their bellies.

The last thing Jinny wanted to do was eat. In fact, she cared not to eat ever again. A couple of the children stood staring at her, so she winked at the youngest, which sent him laughing to his mother. She could hear her sister's irritating voice, but refused to look that direction, and the next thing she knew, Glendon was standing beside her.

Glendon kindly began to introduce Jinny to the members of the clan, and they seemed pleasant enough, although Jinny lost track of their names. Most mentioned their particular talent, the number of children they had, down which path they lived, and then asked about her. Thankfully, she knew how to make baskets, which seemed to please each and every one of them. She wondered, if only briefly, if she should say she was a hunter. After all, hunters could come and go as they pleased, whereas basket makers had to stay in the village. While Glendon was careful not to touch her, some of the women gave her a hug or a pat on the arm in an effort to make her feel welcome.

At length, her husband asked if she wished to eat, but she shook her head and watched him go to the table and fill a bowl for himself.

Though others may have been, Jinny was not at all surprised when Kam and Owena left the celebration. She, on the other hand, was willing to put that particular happenstance off as long as she possibly could. So she stayed, Glendon stayed, and nearly everyone stayed for a time, but then they began to drift away. It became late, and when Glendon nodded for her to come with him, she followed.

CHAPTER 9

IT WAS A SHORT WALK up the slight incline that led to the two cottages she had seen Kam standing in front of. She started to go to it when Glendon motioned for her to enter the other one. He waited for her to open the door and step inside before he went in and closed the door behind them. In the glow of a sun that was nearly down, he said nothing, and instead set about building a small fire in the hearth.

Jinny was surprised to find nearly everything a wife needed, save perhaps a large pot to cook in, plus her personal belongings already in the cottage. Someone had unpacked them, hung her extra clothing on a wooden peg on the wall, and left her hair brush on the table. As well, there was a bowl on the table filled with water in which the tops of several flowers floated.

"'Tis tradition," Glendon said when he noticed her looking at the flowers. "No doubt my sister saw to it while we ate."

"Then I shall thank her, should I ever know which she is."

Glendon smiled for the first time that entire evening. "You shall know her soon enough. She pleases me most, although I'd not like the other sister to know."

"You have my word."

He lit a candle, set it on the table, and then noticed how she had her hands tightly clasped in front of her. "I shall not harm you."

"I know, but..."

"You may have the bed and I shall sleep outside."

She looked as relieved as she felt. "Nay, not outside. 'Tis not for others to know what we do or do not do. You shall sleep in the bed, and I shall sleep on the floor."

"I prefer the floor. Besides, Mother shall ask you if the mattress is soft enough."

At last, Jinny relaxed, pulled a chair away from the table and sat down. She waited until he sat opposite her before she asked, "'Tis true, you meant to marry my sister?"

He moved the flickering candle to one side so he could see her better. "I should not have said that."

"Said what?"

"That I dinna prefer you. I regretted the words as soon as I uttered them."

"'Twas the truth, and I prefer truth over lies." She looked down at her trembling hands, and then laid them in her lap. "I would not have believed you, had you said otherwise. Besides, what is said cannae be unsaid."

"Nay, I suppose not."

She hesitated, but decided to ask again anyway. "You were given first choice and you meant to marry Owena?"

He stared at a knothole in the table trying to find the best way of explaining it. "Aye, but 'twas just as my brother said, Owena clearly preferred him and not me."

Jinny nodded. "I...I hoped...Kam was uncommonly kind to me when I was hurt, and I..."

"Uncommonly? Are the Allaway not kind to you?"

"Some are and some are not." Jinny got up, walked to the bed, sat down and began to take off her shoes. "The truth be told, I hoped Kam would choose me and not Owena."

"I see." It seemed to take a moment for him to accept her confession. "You were against accepting me in the beginning. What changed your mind?"

Jinny supposed he would ask that question eventually, but not quite so soon. "My father convinced me." Next he would ask *how* her father convinced her, and that was the question she truly did not want to answer. Let Glendon and the rest of the MacGreagors find out on their own. Instead, she said, "Forgive me, I tire." She unfolded one of the blankets, set her shoes neatly beside the bed, laid down, and spread the blanket over herself. When Glendon got up and went to her, she held her breath, but all he did was wrap the bottom of the blanket around her feet, then he went back to the table and sat down, this time with his back to her.

GLENDON PUT HIS ELBOW'S on the table and rested his face in his hands. Nothing had turned out the way he intended that morning. It had not been easy letting Kam have his way, but then giving in was never easy for the younger of the two brothers. What worried him more was the look of disbelief on his father's face. Although he did not lie to his father, he feared Ronson suspected there was more to tell, and if asked directly, Glendon would be forced to lie. Lying was something he tried never to do, especially to his father. Once more, Kam had backed Glendon into a corner – one he might not easily get out of.

"Do I never learn?" Glendon whispered.

He closed his eyes and shook his head. Disappointing his father was bad enough, but seeing Owena in Kam's arms made him more resentful than he thought it would. That morning, he was not even certain he wanted to take a wife, even Owena, and now he had one, but the wrong one. Moreover, Jinny had the wrong husband too. It was possible Jinny said that just to even the score, but if true, she had to be just as aggrieved by the outcome of the day as he was. It appeared both of them were condemned to a lifetime of seeing Kam and Owena together.

I am married, he reminded himself as if still unwilling to completely believe it. Jinny seemed less downhearted as time passed. She was clearly unhappy, but she did not cry or display her disappointment in front of the others. For that he was grateful. The less explaining he had to do, the better.

He was surprised when she consented to marry him. He hoped she would not, but once she did, there was no backing out. What did Laird Allaway say or do to convinced Jinny to give in? She said some of the Allaway were unkind to her and the thought gave Glendon reason to pause. Was it possible Laird Allaway threatened to hurt her if she did not comply? If that was the case, then Jinny was not simply convinced, she was forced into the marriage. That was certainly not the way he hoped his marriage would begin.

Glendon finally opened his eyes and sat up a little straighter. He might never find her as pleasing as her sister, but Jinny was his wife and it was up to him to see to her comfort, to protect her, and to hope she might someday accept him of her own free will. At last, he stood up, spread a blanket on the floor, blew the candle out, and went to bed.

SUNRISE CAME EARLY in the MacGreagor glen. Soon, the days would be longer, the garden would yield fresh food, the sheep would need sheering, the wool would be bartered, and all would be well for another year – that is, if it did not rain constantly. Outside, the birds were chirping, the cows mooed to be milked, chickens clucked, and the dogs barked. While Ronson and his wife climbed the hill, the women began the morning by shooing the children outside, and then started to make the daily bread for their families. Men drew in the fresh morning air, grabbed the tool of their choice, or a bucket in which to haul water, and then set out.

All was well outside the two new cottages, but inside was another matter.

When she woke up, Jinny was surprised to see Glendon sitting at the table. Still fully clothed, she shoved the blanket away, sat up, and then reached for her shoes. "Did you not sleep at all?"

"I slept." He turned around and smiled at her. "Are you well?"

"Very," she answered. "Why do you ask? Do you think me unwell?"

"Nay. 'Tis what my father asks my mother when she awakes each mornin'."

"Because he needs her to care for him?"

"Nay, 'tis because he truly cares to know."

She briefly wrinkled her brow and then finished putting on her shoes. Before she went to the table, she went to the shelf, found a mug, and used the dipper to fill it with water from the bucket. "I believe I find comfort in your father's tradition of a mornin'. Are *you* well?"

"Aye." He took a drink from his own mug and waited until she sat down. "Jinny, you must tell me when you are unhappy. There shall be times when..."

"Why? I am here. 'Tis nothin' to be done about it, and my happiness matters not."

"It matters to me."

"Why?"

He looked puzzled by her question. "Because you are my wife and I mean to see that you are well cared for."

"Ah, but well cared for is not the same as bein' happy." She took a drink and then set her mug on the table. Happiness living in the same clan as Owena? Jinny did not believe in miracles. She glanced at the worried look on his face and tried to comfort him with a slight smile. "I have always believed that happiness is practiced, and if practiced well enough, I shall be happy wherever I am." He did not look convinced, so she quickly changed the subject. "What shall I do today? I mean, what does...my husband wish me to do?"

"Well, I am fond of food come the noon sun, and again at supper time."

Jinny giggled. "As am I."

"Other than that, you may please yourself."

"Where do I go to…"

It took a moment for him to realize what she was asking. "Oh, behind the cottage is best." With that, he stood up, nodded, and walked out the door.

At last, she was alone and had a chance to look around. She had a pot to cook in, two wooden bowls, and nearly everything she might need to make a meal. The roof looked sturdy and seemed as though it would not leak when it rained. At least there was no evidence of water stains on the floor, and the walls seemed solid too. Not often did Scotland get a strong wind, but it did happen. The window was small and lacked a curtain, but that was easy to remedy. Moreover, Glendon had taken care to make certain the chairs were smooth and would not yield splinters when she sat. Indeed, it was a fine cottage, and perhaps, just perhaps, she might find some measure of comfort there.

However, what she desired more than comfort was as much peace and quiet as possible before Owena woke up. For that reason, she hurried outside to take care of the particulars, and then slipped back inside her cottage. Her sister was normally a late sleeper, which always pleased the Allaway clan, and Jinny most of all. It usually gave her the better part of the morning to do as she pleased.

It was time to face her new world, so she smoothed the wrinkles out of the skirt, brushed her hair, braided it, and tied the bottom with string. She pulled her shawl off a wooden peg, put it around her shoulders, and stepped outside. To her surprise, three small leather sacks, each tied with string, were positioned together on the ground in front of the door. Jinny glanced around, saw no one, and then noticed there were three small leather sacks in front of the cottage next to hers as well.

When Kam abruptly came out of the other cottage, she caught her breath and stared at him. It was not as though he was frightening, or that she was unprepared to see him again, it meant her sister was living right next door and she had not realized that. "Owena?" she whispered.

It was not a question, but he took it as such. "Aye, she is still sleepin."

Jinny remembered herself and looked down at the small sacks.

"They are spices," said Kam. "A gift to begin your marriage."

"Thank you."

"Nay, thank the lasses."

He looked neither happy nor disturbed, and was on his way down the incline before she could say anything more. She watched him go, and then knelt down and picked up the sacks. Already she could smell the lavender. She took them back inside, found cinnamon in the second bag, and salt in the larger one. It made her sigh. Someday, she would pay the lasses back for their generosity, for she knew full well that her clan shared only what was demanded of them. Her people were not selfish, they were just always short on spices – all the clans were, or so she always thought.

Remembering her urge to escape her sister, she quickly retied the spice strings, slipped back outside and hurried down the incline. At the bottom she stopped, noticed two women watching her, and nodded a greeting. She looked up the glen and then down, spotted the orange and yellow bushes on a hillside farther around the loch, and headed that direction. She would do better to have a basket, but she dinna want to trouble anyone. She could certainly carry as much as she could, go back for more, and then make her own basket. A small berry basket too, and then a basket to carry her washing. Of course, she would not have so much washing to do with just her and Glendon to care for. Not only that, Glendon said she was to please herself and she found making baskets more than pleasing.

Already Jinny had found two advantages to being married that made her happy – at least temporarily. Who knew what her husband would demand of her the day after and the day after that?

The air was a bit crisp as she walked along the path looking for the best heather bushes, but she did not mind. Suddenly, a dog barked behind her. Jinny stopped, turned around, and watched as the dog happily wagged its tale and hurried to greet her. "Well, what be your name?" she asked, kneeling down and rubbing it behind both ears at once. She stood up and then began to shake her finger at the sheep dog. "Why are you not with the herd?" Jinny giggled when the dog tipped its head to one side and then the other. "Very well then, you may come with me."

STANDING IN THEIR USUAL embrace at the top of the hill, Mayzie and Ronson watched. "Jinny pleases you?" Ronson asked his wife.

"Aye."

"And the other one? Owena?"

"Owena dinna climb hills."

Ronson pulled back to look into his wife's laughing eyes. "She dinna climb hills? Never have I known a Scot who dinna love the hills of Scotland."

Mayzie laid her head back against his chest. "How do you suppose Kam convinced Glendon to marry Jinny instead."

"I have given it careful thought and still I cannae imagine."

"Nor can I. Glendon dinna appear to resent his brother for talkin' him out of it, but does Glendon not always hide is feelings well?"

"Aye." Mayzie watched Jinny play with the dog again and sighed. "If he is resentful, I fear life might be a bit more tryin' in the MacGreagor glen for a time."

"True," he muttered. "I should have requested daughters instead."

She giggled, and then wiped a smudge off his cheek. "Too late."

COLLECTING FALLEN BRANCHES on an adjacent hillside, Glendon paused to watch his wife as she playfully pushed the dog away so she could cut and gather more heather. It wasn't working. At length, Jinny tried a different tactic. She tossed a branch away for the dog to fetch. When the dog brought it back and would not let go, she dropped her bundle and began a tug-of-war with it. The dog growled, Jinny laughed, and when the dog abruptly let go, Jinny landed in the tall grass on her backside.

Jinny MacGreagor's laughter seemed to echo through the glen and her husband was not the only one watching. When he looked, several others were too including his parents, and they were all smiling. Just then, the dog rushed forward, pounced on top of Jinny tried to lick her in the face, and even then she continued to laugh.

It was the last truly peaceful moment Glendon would have that day, for when Kam walked through the trees to find his brother, it had already begun.

"Mornin.'"

"For you, perhaps." Kam muttered.

Glendon was amazed. "You are not happy?"

"She prefers to sleep of a mornin', or so she says."

"Oh." It was just like Kam to want what he wanted in the moment, and then find fault with it later. Yet, unlike other things that did not eventually suit Kam, Owena was not something he could easily dismiss. Glendon tried not to pay any attention to his brother, and he might have been successful, but before he could gather two more branches, he heard a woman scream his brother's name.

"KAM! KAM, I AM IN NEED OF MORE WATER!"

Glendon watched his brother out of the corner of his eye. Kam had not moved, nor did it appear he intended to.

"KAM!" Owena shouted again.

This time, Glendon looked at his wife. Even though the dog still meant to pester her, Jinny was looking up the incline at her sister, and seemed unable to move. Between the trees, he could just barely see Owena standing in front of Kam's cottage and – she was wearing nothing but her underclothing.

Kam puffed his cheeks, tossed a frustrated glance at his brother, and then headed home. As soon as he was gone, Glendon moved away from the trees so he could better see what Kam would do. He watched his brother walk up the incline, pick Owena up, put her over his shoulder, and then hauled her back inside. Instead of being angered by it, Owena thought it was funny and began to laugh. Unlike her sister's pleasant laughter, Owena exhibited a piercing sort of sound he had never heard before.

Again he looked at his wife. Jinny had bowed her head.

"WELL," SAID MAYZIE as she hugged her husband one last time. "Best I settle our new daughters-in-law, and show them where everythin' is."

Ronson released her, watched her start down the hill and then waited to see if Kam would come back out and tend to his chores. It took a few minutes, but Kam finally appeared. He looked a bit bewildered, and in his hand was the empty water bucket. Ronson watched his son fetch water from the loch, carry it up the hill, and then go back inside. "Perhaps she is unwell," he muttered. He shrugged, and then walked down the hill to check the new growth of the garden.

By then, Mayzie had made it to Jinny. She sent the dog away, and then began to help Jinny collect heather stems. Jinny seemed distant and uncommonly quiet, but Mayzie could understand why. At length, she asked, "What shall you make first?"

"Baskets," Jinny replied. "I shall make a berry basket first, and then a larger one for the wash. Or perhaps I should make a large one for the wash first. Do you wash in the loch or is there a creek nearby?"

"In the shallow part of the loch. I shall show you where 'tis safest."

Jinny pause in her stem collecting and stood up straight. "Whom do I thank for the spices?"

"'Tis kept secret."

"Why?"

"Because we know well what 'tis like to begin anew in an unfamiliar place, and with a husband we know not how to please. 'Tis enough just to know we have helped."

Jinny wrinkled her brow for a moment and then nodded. "And therefore, those who could not contribute, are not made to feel unworthy when the bride thanks the ones that could?"

"Precisely."

"I wonder...shall I find some of the MacGreagors to be of ill temper?"

"I have never thought so. My sons dinna see eye-to-eye sometimes, but..."

"Then Kam shall not hurt my sister?"

The expression on Mayzie's face was one of astonishment. "Never! 'Tis forbidden for a MacGreagor husband to harm his wife. Glendon shall not harm you either."

Jinny contemplated that for a moment and then went back to cutting heather stems. She hesitated to ask, but it had been on her mind. "May I know about the MacGreagor curse? Kam said 'tis folly, but others say differently."

"Kam is right. Many years hence, there came a drought. The MacGreagors of old came here in search of water and when 'twas found, Bearnard took off his shirt and waded in. That began the gossip for there were those that saw the mark for themselves."

"They say all the animals died because of his mark, but I dinna believe it."

Mayzie giggled. "We have heard that too. You have seen the tree?"

"I have. My mother fears the MacGreagors are not healthy."

Mayzie had not heard that rumor. "In what way?"

"I know not, you look healthy enough to me, more so than some others I have seen."

"Well, perhaps someday your mother might come to see for herself."

"She likely shall."

"If we have gathered enough heather, let us take it to your cottage, and then I shall show you to the cellars. We have six of them, two of which are hidden in the trees so that other clans cannae find them if we are attacked." They were halfway back to the village when Mayzie said, "We best fetch your sister, so I may show her as well."

Jinny was afraid of that.

After they put the heather stems inside her cottage and went back outside, Jinny did her best not to look distressed about having to knock on Owena's door. When Owena did not answer, Jinny glanced at Mayzie and smiled. She thought to say Owena was hard of hearing, but everyone would soon know that was not true. She forced herself to look happy and knocked again.

At last, Owena opened the door. She was still not dressed, her hair was a mess, and as usual, it did not appear that she cared who saw her. "Jinny, you have come finally. What kept you?"

"Owena," Jinny tried, "Mayzie is with me and wishes to show us..."

"I hardly can go out today sister. I suffer twice the unhappiness I feared." She opened the door wider, and looked to see where Mayzie was. "'Tis hardly livable here. I've nothin' – nay, nothin' at all with which to please myself. We've only one bench to sit on, the mattress is lumpy and too hard, and..."

"Sister," Jinny quickly interrupted, "you are mistaken. I found the bed far softer than the one we had at home."

"Perhaps so, but..."

"Owena," Jinny interrupted again. "You best come see where to find everythin'."

Owena whined. "I cannae, I am unwell. Can you not show me tomorrow?"

Jinny drew in a deep breath. "Very well, I shall show you tomorrow."

"Good day then," said Owena as she closed the door in Jinny's face.

Jinny hung her head for a moment, and then pretended it did not matter. She put her brave face back on and went to join Mayzie. Neither of them mentioned the encounter, mainly because Jinny could not think what to say. She had spent her life apologizing for her sister, and it only brought pity on herself. Jinny finally said. "I am determined to be happy here no matter the circumstances."

"'Tis what I decided when I first came. Happiness will come to you, Jinny, I am certain of it. All good things come once we have accepted the life that is to be."

Jinny was far from certain of that, but there was hope. There was always hope.

First, Mayzie showed her to the cellars. There was just enough light coming in from outside for both of them to see. "When the elder's pass, we put their things here to be used by the next generation." She picked up a medium size pot and handed it to Jinny. "I know not what Glendon chose for you, but this one is likely better. I suggest you give the pot a good scrubbin."

"Then I best make a scrub brush first."

Mayzie smiled. "Good. Of the food, take what you need. Glendon is a hearty eater and..."

"As is my father. I shall see that he does not go hungry." She spotted a hand cleaver on a table she could use later to chop off a chunk of meat from the deer carcass that hung from the roof. The vegetable bins were nearly empty, but there were a few white carrots, several heads of cabbage and some onions. It would be enough, she decided.

"I feel certain we shall have fresh vegetables in a day or two. Come, and I shall show you where to get string for tyin' your heather." Mayzie waited until they were back up top, closed the door and then turned to Jinny. "When you come back, take enough for your sister and Kam. If she is unwell, perhaps she...?"

"I shall see to them," Jinny quickly interrupted. Owena was quite capable of making a meal, not that she ever felt the need. As usual she refrained from criticizing her sister. What was the point? The MacGreagors would soon see how completely useless her sister truly was. Owena was just a handsome face and little else.

On the other side of the village, Mayzie knocked on the door of a cottage and waited for Rossalyn to answer.

"Ah, Mayzie and Jinny," Rossalyn said greeting them. "Come in."

"Rossalyn is our laird's sister," Mayzie said, "and our best weaver." She went on to explain, "Jinny makes baskets and is in need of string."

Rossalyn unwound string from a ball, measured a length from the tip of her finger to her shoulder, cut it, and then handed the length to Jinny. "Shall we not trade string for a new basket? Our best basket weaver passed in winter, and some try making them, but they have not yet mastered it."

Jinny quickly nodded. "What size basket do you desire?"

"The weaver pointed at a dilapidated basket on the floor filled with balls of wool yarn. Jinny set the empty pot aside, knelt down to feel the stiffness of the heather, nodded and got up. "This can be mended, but a new one would do better."

"A new one would greatly please me." Rossalyn took hold of Mayzie's hand. "I hear Old Shep likes her, so I say we keep this one."

"Old Shep?" Jinny asked.

"The dog you played with this mornin." Rosslyn answered. "Old Shep dinna fancy just anyone, but he fancies you. Glendon has chosen well for himself."

"I agree," said Mayzie. "Indeed, we must keep this one."

Jinny looked perplexed. "Have you sent many a bride back?"

"None yet," Mayzie answered, as she opened the door and waited until Jinny passed through. She winked at the weaver and then closed the door.

For Jinny, maybe there was more hope than she thought. How fitting it would be if the MacGreagors sent Owena back to the Allaway and kept her with them? Jinny had never heard of such a thing, but there were rumors about the MacGreagors and their strange ways. Maybe that was one of them. Hope, a flicker of it, had just been ignited.

CHAPTER 10

JINNY WAS ANYTHING but eager to prepare a meal for her sister and Kam, but it was what Mayzie asked her to do, so she set her mind to it. After cleaning, putting the pot Mayzie gave her, and the string she gained from Rosslyn in her cottage, she went next door. Certain Kam was not home, she did not bother to knock, slipped inside her sister's cottage and was relieved to find that Owena had gone back to bed. She liked Owena best when she was sleeping. Surprised that Kam had not sufficiently supplied the necessities for his wife the way Glendon had, she took stock of what was needed, quietly left, and then went back to the cellar.

An hour later, after seeking what could be had in three cellars and waiting in line while other wives got what they needed, Jinny knocked on Owena's door. In her arms she carried bowls, cups, spoons, a wooden ladle, and a second cleaned pot filled with enough food for her sister and Kam's supper. The sun was rising high in the sky, and it would surely take the rest of the day to sufficiently cook the raw food, but that was not what concerned Jinny most. There was little she could do about the noon meal for either couple. Two meals a day was all that Glendon requested of her, and already she had no choice but to disappoint him. She looked back toward the village, did not see her husband, and sighed. He would be furious and she did not blame him.

Frustrated and resentful of her sister's pretending to be unwell, Jinny loudly knocked on the door again, only this time louder.

Owena was stretched out on the bed, and hardly lifted her head enough to bid her visitor to come in.

"Owena, get up!" Jinny commanded, as she pulled the door closed behind her. "I care not to have you shame me in front of the MacGreagors."

"What do I care if you are shamed? Never have I been so miserable." She lazily turned over and closed her eyes.

Jinny set the pot on the table, felt how lopsided it was, and hung on to the pot handle for fear the table might tip over. Just in case, she moved the pot to the center to balance the weight and carefully let go. Then she glared at her sister. "If you wish to eat supper this night, you shall give me your pledge, and give it this very moment!"

"Kam will see that I have my supper. He is my husband now, and 'tis his duty."

"I wonder that he knows that," Jinny muttered. The fire in the hearth was about to go out, so she went outside, got a medium size log from the wood pile, and brought it back inside. She set it down in front of the hearth, rolled it into the fire, and then stood back to see if it would begin to burn. When it did, she added water and salt to the pot, and then carefully hung the handle on the hook over the fire. "There. See that it dinna burn. 'Tis the least you can do."

Owena finally sat up. "Sister, what am I to do? I cannae go home, for Father shall not allow it. How shall I suffer a lifetime of being Kam's wife?"

"Is that not what you wanted yesterday? Aye, it is, and now that I am forced to live with your misery as well, know this: 'Tis the last meal I shall ever make for you and your husband."

"You dinna mean that. You cannae. I am to be the next mistress, and then you shall be forced to make a meal for us when I command it." She got up, went to the fire and peeked into the pot. "Is there no bread? I hunger now."

Jinny rolled her eyes, opened the door and walked out. Soon, she was in her own home, doing the same thing with the pot full of food she had fetched for her and Glendon. Bread was a problem. She knew how to make it; she just hadn't noticed where to find the ingredients. Besides, she had no flat pan to make it on. She supposed she should go back to the cellar and have another look around. When the door abruptly opened, Jinny's whole body involuntarily shook. With wide eyes, she rushed to the opposite side of the room, and spun around to face her intruder.

"Forgive me," said Glendon as he set something wrapped in cloth on the table. "I dinna mean to frighten you. I shall knock first in future."

She took a deep breath, and forced herself to calm down. He did not look angry, though he surely could tell she had nothing to feed him. "'Tis nearly noon. I should have expected you."

"Jinny, it is forbidden for a MacGreagor to hurt a woman or a child. You are safe here, even from me."

He looked sincere when he said it, and it was what his mother said too, but still... She nodded her understanding and walked to the opposite side of the table.

"Mother sees that you are busy and sent fresh bread and cheese for our noon meal. Sit."

She filled two wooden cups with water, set them on the table, sat, unwrapped the cloth and was delighted to see what was inside. There was a large portion of both. She had not realized it, but she had not eaten since the previous morning and she was hungry. Jinny did not bother putting the food in a bowl. Instead, she waited for him to cut the cheese, take a chunk of bread in one hand, and cheese in the other, before she helped herself.

The two of them ate in silence for a time, he eager to fill his stomach, and she still too timid to eat much for fear he was not yet contented. At length, she said, "Your mother is most kind to me."

"Aye, she is a good lass. Most lasses are good, although some are kinder than others. Kindness is a gift."

"True, but everyone has a gift to give of some kind."

"They do," he agreed. "Yet, are some gifts not well hidden?"

She looked at the glint in his eye. Was it possible her husband was wise enough to already suspect the truth about her sister? It appeared so. "Aye. Some are hidden far better than you suppose."

He grinned, shoved the last bite of his share of food in his mouth, chewed, swallowed, and then washed it down with water. "I mean to build a fire pit outside soon, so you are not forced to cook inside on days that are too hot, and in winter, I shall build proper chairs."

"I shall like that very much."

"What else are you in need of on this day."

"I can think of nothing just now." She watched him stand up, walk to the door, opened it, and then turn around before he left. "Come find me if you are in need. I shall be cutting wood not far from where you gathered heather."

"I shall." Jinny went to the window and watched him walk down the incline. He also meant, she supposed, when he said about the gifts that the clan was already wondering about Owena's slothfulness. She was expecting that and it was a useless thing to fret over. Besides, her concern now had to do with the true nature of her husband. He seemed kind, caring, and unusually concerned for her wellbeing. He was not like the Allaway men at all, and although she tried not to be, she was suspicious of Glendon's motives.

A shrill shout from the cottage next door interrupted her thoughts. "JINNY, I HUNGER!"

Horrified, she sharply inhaled. Everyone in view was looking her direction, and Glendon had turned completely around. She quickly moved away from the window, put her back against the wall, and tried to think what to do. Ignoring Owena never worked. She would continue to shout until she got her way, and if Jinny did nothing, the

MacGreagors would be forced to endure it. Instead, she wrapped what was left of the bread and cheese back up, walked out, knocked on Owena's door, and opened it. She stood in the doorway with one hand on her hip. "Owena, I shall thank you not to yell for me!"

Owena curled her bottom lip into a pout. "I hunger, Kam brings me nothing to eat, and the stew is not yet cooked."

Jinny set the cloth on the table, and then took a step back. "And your husband? What is he to eat?"

"I care not what Kam does. 'Twas he who brought me to this misery."

About that, Jinny had to agree. They were both there because of Kam. "Aye, but 'tis you who casts your misery on *me*."

Owena glared. "I shall be your mistress someday,"

"But not yet. Can you not allow me some measure of happiness until then?"

"Happiness? You suppose *you* shall be happy while I suffer? I find that most selfish of you."

Jinny turned around and went back to the door. "Of course you do." She walked out, closed the door and went home, all the while refusing to look to see if anyone was watching her. If they were and she witnessed it, her embarrassment would be complete.

In years gone by, when she'd had enough of her sister's demands, she would slam a door, and then curtsy to anyone who happened to be watching. She thought to do the same just now, but she knew not how strangers would react to it. At least she was proud of herself for laying down the law to her overbearing sister. Never again would she do the cooking or anything else for Owena. On that subject, she made to herself a solemn vow!

There was only one thing wrong. Owena had a way of riling her and it usually took time for Jinny to calm down. Making baskets was delicate work and rushed, the work never measured up to her high standards. Not only that, she had not eaten much and was still hungry.

No need to fret over that now. She grabbed an arm full of heather stems, set them on the table, and then found the string where she left it.

First, she carefully set the small heather flowers aside so she could boil them with honey into a broth that was good for coughs, a nervous stomach, the stiffness of bones, and whatever else made people feel ill at ease. A paste made of heather helped sooth sunburns, bee stings, and some even thought a drink or two of heather water helped a sleepless rest. She heard somewhere that mixing heather flowers in it, made soap smell glorious. Jinny was determined to try that the next time she needed to make soap.

She had just finished removing the flowers, set several stems in a row, and was ready to cut them with her knife when someone knocked on the door. Her impulse was to turn the knife around to protect herself. Instead she laid it down. "Come in."

Glendon was back and he did not look pleased. He handed her another cloth containing bread and cheese, and then said, "So long as I live, *my* wife shall not go hungry – nay, not even for her sister's sake."

"Glendon, I..."

"Eat!" he said, walking out and closing the door behind him.

She stared at the purple heather stems on the table for a moment, pushed them aside, sat down and filled her stomach complete. To her, the taste was more than heavenly. The MacGreagors, it appeared, liked a better portion of salt in their cheese than the Allaway.

When she finished, there was enough left to save for later, so she put it on the shelf and returned to the table. First, she closely wove and knotted the stems together to make a basket base, leaving enough length to begin the sides. It was sometimes difficult work knotting the stems, and when she first learned it was painful. Now, however, she had calluses where it mattered most, and she had learned how to avoid hurting her fingers.

When she checked the stew, she used the ladle to taste it, added a little more water, more salt and a pinch more lavender. Soon, her home smelled like home.

JINNY CHECKED TO MAKE certain the embers in the hearth glowed enough to keep her supper simmering, grabbed the nearly empty bucket, and opened the door. To her amazement, a young girl sat on a nearby log waiting for her.

Instantly the girl got up. "I am Bradana, Glendon's sister. He sent me to see if you wished anything. Of course, I would have come soon anyway, but mother says I'm not to pester you so soon after you arrived. You are Jinny are you not? I wished for a name like Jinny, but it was not to be. Father chose all our names, and mother had not a thing to say about it."

Jinny smiled at her chatterbox new friend. "I am happy to meet you. Perhaps you might show me where 'tis the best place to fetch water."

"'Tis but a short walk. 'Tis much farther from our cottage, but then, the laird's cottage was built long ago, before I was born even." She started down the incline, and then glanced back to make certain Jinny was coming.

"Glendon says I have you to thank for seeing to my belongings and for the bowl of flowers. It pleased me very much."

Bradana paused to wait for Jinny to catch up. "Do you find marriage to your liking? My mother thinks you are the best wife for Glendon. She says little of your sister. Everyone save mother is talking of Owena, and..."

Jinny was about to quickly change the subject when the mule started to bray. Instead of munching on the grass in the shade of a pine tree, it appeared to be looking at her. "Not often have I seen a mule."

"That's Calla. We know not from where she came. One day, she just came walkin' up the glen, and as you can see, she has yet to go home."

"Tis a she mule?"

"Father says so, but she cannae have offspring. I know not why."

"Perhaps 'tis just as well."

"True, we dinna need more Callas." When they neared the loch, Bradana led Jinny down a path alongside the water, until she came to an inlet of sorts where the rocks along the shore were smooth and easy to stand on. "Might you teach me to make baskets?"

"I'd be happy to."

"Mother says, there never be enough basket makers."

They were almost halfway to the water when Jinny noticed a young boy who seemed unable to take his eyes off her. "Who might that be?" she asked, nodding toward the boy.

"Oh, that be Cerdic."

"I believe I have seen him before."

Bradana sighed, "He be a bother, but harmless. Mother says he seeks excitement no matter the cost to the clan or the sheep." She slowly lifted a hand and waved to Cerdic, which made the young boy realize he'd been seen, quickly rush off, and disappear into the heart of the village.

Jinny carefully walked across the rocks, and then gathered her skirt so she would not get it wet. Just as she dipped her bucket in the water, she heard the shrieking sound of Owena's voice.

"JINNY!"

Jinny jerked the half-full bucket back out of the water and let go of her skirt. The water splashed down the front of her, but that was not the worst of her problems. For a moment, she thought her sister was right behind her, and even though the rocks were smooth, when she tried to quickly turn around she almost lost her balance. At last, she righted herself and looked back. That Owena was not right behind her and instead was standing in her cottage doorway horrified Jinny even more. The shape of the glen had somehow magnified her sister's voice, causing those near and far to stop, turn, look at Owena... and then at her.

Jinny wanted to die.

"There she goes again," said Bradana. Next, Calla renewed her braying. "Not you too," she moaned.

Just that morning Jinny swore not to be at her sister's beck and call, but what else could she do? It was a useless vow, it always was. Thoroughly humiliated, Jinny carried the half bucket of water up the hill. By then, Owena had gone back inside, so Jinny set the bucket down on a level place on the ground, and then knocked on her door just before she shoved it wide open. "What?"

"I thirst and our bucket is empty. Can I not have some of *your* water?"

"Can you not get *your own* water?" She pointed behind her. "The loch is down there."

"Aye, but I am very tired – so tired, I can hardly move."

Jinny glanced back and was further humiliated to find that several had gathered to see if there would be another spectacle, like the one earlier when Owena neglected to dress. Among them was Glendon and his little sister. Apparently, Bradana had gone to be with her brother, and just now he had his arm around her as if to comfort her. Glendon, Jinny noticed, did not look happy and she did not blame him.

At least Calla had quieted, which was a relief.

Jinny went back for the bucket, and then carried it inside Owena's cottage. A few seconds later, she emerged with an empty bucket and started back down the incline. She was so upset, when she turned back down the path, she dinna even notice Glendon coming right behind her. It was not until she gathered her skirt again, that she felt him take hold of the bucket handle. Surprised, she turned to look at him. This time, his expression was one of pity.

There it was finally, the second worst thing in the world. The first was Owena, and the second was seeing pity on the faces of people who felt sorry for Jinny. Now, even her husband pitied her. Soon she would see it in many a MacGreagor expression. Oh well, they would get used to it, she guessed. Jinny let go of the handle and then watched as he walked across the rocks and refilled the bucket for her.

When he came back, he asked, "Is your sister prone to often shout for you?"

"I suppose 'tis too late to lie and say it happens but seldom. Where is Kam?" she asked, displaying a little more hostility than she meant to.

"He's gone huntin'."

Jinny looked away. "Do the MacGreagors allow lasses to go huntin'?"

He slowly smiled. "Surely you dinna mean you wish to go huntin' *without* your sister."

She could not help but return his grin, if only slightly, before she sarcastically said, "I'd not dream of it."

"I thought not. Perhaps my brother can speak to his wife about her shouting."

"'Twill do no good. Father has tried every possible remedy and still she..." Jinny stopped talking and looked away again.

"Jinny, tell me true. What did your father say to persuade you to marry me?"

"He said..." she started, and then changed her mind.

"Go on, tell me. I give you my pledge – what you say shall go no further."

At length, she decided to answer. "Father said she would soon shame the Allaway if she did not marry, and if he was not shed of her, he would surely die before his time."

Glendon set the bucket down, folded his arms and took a moment to ponder what she said. "And Owena would not marry unless you married me." When Jinny hung her head, he cast his eyes downward too. After a time, he said, "Come." He picked the bucket back up and started for home. "Perhaps I might persuade my brother to take to a cottage on the other side of the village."

"Aye, but 'twould be farther for me to go when she shouts." He said no more, and she did not expect him to. There was no answer to the problem of Owena. If there was, she would have found it years ago. Her father often attempted to handle his strong-willed daughter, but instead of complying, Owena always became even more rebellious. In the end, Laird Allaway simply threw up his hands and gave up the fight.

Owena was...well just Owena.

WHEN HE CAME HOME FOR supper that evening, Glendon did not say much except that her cooking pleased him. It was not until after she cleaned up, after he let the fire go out, and after she lay down on the bed, that he spread his blanket on the floor and sat down on it. "Tomorrow, William and I shall go on the hunt. The clan is in need of more meat."

She wanted to ask if Kam had come home, and if so, did he intend to do something about Owena, but she decided against it. Time would answer that question. "Good hunting, then," was all she said, but then she remembered a question she meant to ask him. "Glendon, when I was in the Lennox village, a lass was most kind to me. I wish to befriend her. Are the MacGreagors forbidden to visit the Lennox?"

"Nay, 'tis the Lennox who do the forbidding. They fear a MacGreagor shall marry a Lennox and thereby carry the curse to them as well. Now that you are married, they shall have no cause to deny you."

In the dim light of the fading fire, Jinny sighed. "The MacGreagors may not have thought themselves cursed before – but they are now." Exhausted, she turned her back to him. Her first day as a MacGreagor had its good moments and its bad. At least Glendon would be gone the next day, and therefore not be put upon to witness her sister's nonsense.

It would get worse before it got better – if it ever got better.

CHAPTER 11

EARLY THE NEXT MORNING, Glendon woke Jinny. "Promise you shall ask Mother if you are in need while I am gone."

"I promise," she said, pushing herself up to a sitting position.

He had only been gone for a few minutes before it began. Someone, and she did not have to imagine who, was throwing things against the wall in the cottage next door. "Owena," she sadly whispered.

Alone in her new home, she wiped the sleep from her eyes, got up, and changed into her spare clothing. She normally wore her undergarments to bed, but she was not yet comfortable enough around Glendon to do that. She gathered the ones she had been sleeping in, examined Glendon's spare clothing, and decided his were still clean enough. Probably, Mayzie had washed them when she knew Glendon was about to take a wife.

With the clothes still in her arms, and after she heard another bang likely from something else thrown against the wall next door, she stepped outside just in time to see Kam backing out of his cottage. He looked astonished as he ducked to avoid a flying wooden bowl.

As if reminding himself, he said, "'Tis forbidden for a lad to hurt a lass – even *that* lass!" When he noticed Jinny, he shook his head, and then ran down the incline.

"KAM!" Owena screamed. By the time she came to the door to look for him, he had gone completely out of sight. It was then she spotted Jinny. "Sister, what am I to do? Never have I known such misery."

"Not since yesterday," Jinny muttered. Apparently, Kam made his wife get up and get dressed. That was something, at least.

Owena's demeanor completely changed when she saw the clothing in Jinny's arms. "Oh good, 'tis wash day." She hurried back inside and when she came out, she added several items to her sister's load.

"You care not to do your own washing now that you are married?"

"Why should I? Are you not doing yours anyway?"

Somehow, Owena's excuses always had a touch of truth to them. There was no point in arguing, especially because it meant that Owena would not be screaming for her. Her sister was at least wise enough not to bother Jinny when she was doing Owena's bidding.

The night before, Jinny decided to give in and be servant to her sister just to keep Owena quiet. It was the least she could do for a clan that had welcomed her as kindly as the MacGreagors had. Many a story had she heard of brides being scorned by the husband's clan when they thought he married unwisely. It was in an effort to keep Owena quiet that Jinny said, "Perhaps we might go for a walk later."

"A walk? Where to? I see nothing of interest in this dreary old glen."

"I had hoped to see the Lennox village again."

Owena's eyes instantly lit up. "Aye, I should like to visit the Lennox again too. They have some very handsome lads in the..."

"Owena, you are married."

"Sister, dinna remind me. 'Tis the worst thing in the world to wake up, and know you have been forced to marry so unwisely."

"Forced?"

"Aye, forced. As you are well aware, I hoped to be in love when I married. I could never love a lad like Kam. He sees not to my needs at all, and has condemned me to a life of unthinkable desolation."

"I see," Jinny mumbled. There was no use pointing out that it was Owena who forced Jinny to marry. Not in a thousand years would Owena admit it, not to herself, and certainly not to Jinny. She heaved a sigh of relief when her sister went back inside and closed her door. Remembering what she forgot, she went back into her cottage, grabbed the bar of soap, and then went off to do her wash.

IT TURNED OUT TO BE a very busy day. Jinny did the wash, found some tree limbs near her cottage to hang the clothes on while they dried, and then found the ingredients for making bread, and two small rolls of cheese in one of the cellars. Though a little lopsided, she discovered a pot that would do. It was flat enough on the bottom with short walls perfect for making bread. She scrubbed the pan with soap and a heather scrub brush she quickly made the evening before, and then cooked enough flat cakes for herself, her sister, and Kam. Jinny was proud of herself. She managed to deliver the noon meal before Owena thought to yell for her. Next, she went home and quickly ate. Her bread needed a little more salt, but she could remedy that the next time she made it.

As soon as Kam left, she hurried next door, picked up the bowl Owena threw at Kam, and then went inside to see what remained of the supper she had made for her sister the day before. There was nothing left, so she took the pot and the bucket of water outside so she could clean it, and then went back to the cellars to get enough food for four suppers. All the while, she had a frown on her face, and made no eye contact with anyone. Nevertheless, there were those watching.

At home, she cut a rabbit carcass in half, divided the cabbage, onions, and turnips, and then put an equal portion in each pot. She carried Owena's pot next door, hung it over the smoldering embers, added water and spices, and then went outside to find more wood. Back inside, she set the wood down, and then turned to her sister.

"If you are going for a walk with me, you best brush your hair."

"Oh, aye," Owena said. She climbed out of bed, and while she searched for where she had last thrown her brush, Jinny slipped out the door.

Home at last and nearly exhausted. Jinny had just enough burning wood left in her hearth to bring her pot of food to a boil, therefore allowing it to cook while she went to visit the Lennox. An untended fire of any good size was dangerous, but she thought herself careful enough, and back soon enough to avoid the problem. She added plenty of water, her spices, and then sat down at the table to rest. Hopefully, it would take Owena a few minutes to become presentable. It always did, and occasionally, it took more than an hour, which on this day would suit Jinny just fine.

Naturally, it was not to be, and instead of coming to her door and knocking, Owena stayed outside and yelled, "JINNY!"

Jinny puffed her cheeks and stood up. She checked the fire once more, and then went to join her sister. "You need not yell at me, I can hear you just fine, even inside my cottage."

"Do not rebuke me Jinny. My life is dreadful enough as it is."

Jinny rolled her eyes, closed her door, and once more started down the incline.

Owena was happy finally, so Jinny pretended to be as well. She stopped beside the garden, asked two of the boys their names, and committed them to memory. Three other children were busy trying to keep Calla from eating the tops off of the vegetables, so she was careful not to distract them. Even then, she did not acknowledge the adult members of the clan. She was just too humiliated by her sister's behavior to face them.

From the garden, they walked the distance to the stonewall, carefully climbed over it and then found the path to the Lennox village. On the outskirts of the busy village, they stopped. The Lennox, the ones who noticed them first, seemed surprised to see them. Soon others noticed and they too stopped to stare at them. At last, the girl who had been kind to Jinny two days earlier waved and then came to greet her. Jinny was relieved.

"I am happy to see you again," said Aila Lennox. "Have you come to see father?"

"Nay, I came to see you." Jinny motioned to Owena. "My sister and I are now married to brothers, Kam and Glendon MacGreagor."

"Kam is married?" Aila asked. "I wager a few of our lasses shall be saddened to hear that."

"Tell them not to be," Owena sneered, "He is not but a burdensome bother."

Aila giggled, "'Tis a happy marriage then."

Owena missed the sarcasm completely. "Hardly." Not but a moment later, she spotted a Lennox lad watching her, and smiled at him. "Who might he be?"

Aila turned to see who Owena was talking about. "That be Gerwin."

"Gerwin Lennox is handsome indeed," said Owena.

"Might I remind you," Jinny said, "you are married."

"Am I? I've not seen Kam this whole day complete."

Jinny would have mentioned why, but not in front of her new friend. Instead she asked Aila, "Why do they stare at us?"

Aila glanced back at the people in the village. "Oh," she said. She cupped her hands around her mouth and shouted, "THEY ARE MARRIED!" That was all it took for most of the Lennox to go back to doing their chores.

"Still think the MacGreagors cursed?" Jinny asked.

"Most have seen no proof of it, but..." Aila tried.

"I say they *are* cursed," Owena whined.

"We," Jinny reminded her sister. "We are MacGreagors now too," She was relieved when it appeared Aila would continue to ignore her sister, and paid more attention to her instead.

"Do you wish to see how the puppies have grown?" Aila asked Jinny.

"Very much," Jinny replied.

Owena huffed. "Puppies, do the MacGreagors not have puppies for you to look upon? Aye, they do. I care not to see them. I care not at all."

Jinny was more than pleased. "Then stay here while I go." She did not wait for her sister's reply before she began to walk with Aila toward the village. When she looked back, Owena had put on her lost little girl face, and was slightly swinging her hips. Next, Jinny glanced at Gerwin Lennox to see if he was watching. Of course he was watching. Not only that, he had already started to walk toward Owena.

Coming had been a bad idea, she could see that now. A lad could get killed for flirting with another lad's wife, and Jinny knew that very well. She had seen the anger in a man's eyes once before in the Allaway village. In that instance, neither man died, but Jinny hoped never to see such a frightening display as that again.

Abruptly, Jinny stopped. The thought that Kam might find out, and that the battle between two men could lead to a clan war was more than she could bear. Instead of walking back, she began to run. As soon as she reached her, she grabbed Owena's arm and turned her around. "We must go back."

"NAY!" Owena shouted.

"I am ill, sister."

"Nay, 'tis just an excuse."

"I fear I might soon soil myself!"

"Oh, that kind of ill." Owena looked back at the man she hoped to make the acquaintance of, noticed he had stopped coming toward her, and sighed. "Very well, we shall come again tomorrow."

"If I am able," Jinny huffed.

"Do you suppose it is catching? I care not to fall ill because of you."

"I know not."

Even then, Owena had no intention of walking any faster than she had when they arrived. Thankfully, Jinny had lied about her health, but if her sister believed her, perhaps she might let her be for the rest of the afternoon. It had worked in the past. Just to make certain, when they got home Jinny rushed around to the back of her cottage.

When she returned, Mayzie had somehow convinced Owena to go with her, probably to the cellars. Jinny cringed at the thought that her sister would insult the MacGreagor mistress, but there was nothing she could do about that. She slipped inside Owena and Kam's cottage, checked the stew and the fire, and then went home.

By the time she went inside her own cottage, she noticed someone had retrieved her dry laundry, shook everything out and hung the things on the pegs for her, although whoever it was did not know the difference between her clothing and Owena's. Relieved of that chore, she glanced out the window to make certain her sister was not in sight, and quickly took Owena's things next door.

At last, she was alone. Any other time, she would have liked being outside, and even working on a basket outside, but on this day she was grateful for the solitude being inside promised. She checked her own stew, sat down on the bed, and took a moment just to breathe and relax.

JINNY WAS SOUND ASLEEP when Glendon came home, and at the knock on the door, she abruptly sat up. Distressed that she had fallen asleep, she quickly stood, pushed the loose strands of hair off her face, and said, "Come in."

"Tis just me."

"Good hunting?" she asked as she watched him close the door.

"Very good, we brought back two red deer and four rabbits." He took off his cloak, hung it on a peg, and then turned to her. "I hear you have worked your fingers to the bone this day."

"Nay, I am fine."

"You are not ill? Owena told Mother you..."

Jinny released a held breath. "I lied to my sister." She was surprised when Glendon smiled.

"Good for you." He undid the strings of his sword and hung that up as well. "Jinny, why do you feel you must care for your sister?"

"I..." She tried to buy time to think, by grabbing the ladle, going to the supper pot, and stirring it. "I cannae abide her screaming. I never could. And twice more, I cannae let her plague your people by allowing it."

"They are your people now. Do you intend to remain slave to your sister forever?"

"If needs be." She avoided his piercing eyes, tasted the stew broth, and decided it needed a touch more salt. Jinny was about to reach for the salt sack when he took hold of her hand.

Her eyes finally met his, and when they did she looked terrified. Glendon quickly let go. "What is it, Jinny? Why are you frightened of me?"

"I...perhaps I shan't be once I know you better."

"I hope so." To ease her mind, he pulled a stool away from the table and sat down. "Tell me, what are we to do about your sister's demands?"

She grabbed a bowl, filled it with steaming hot rabbit stew, picked up a spoon, and set both in front of him. "Did I not tell you before? There is nothing to be done. I know of no remedy, no threat she fears, no sufficient punishment, nor do I even have a suggestion. We have tried everythin'." She filled a bowl for herself, got a spoon, and then sat opposite him.

"There must be something."

Jinny stared into his eyes for a moment. "What does Kam say?"

"Kam knows not what to say or do." He dipped his spoon in the broth, blew on it, and then sipped the contents of the spoon. "I hope Kam enjoys his supper as much as I enjoy mine, for it is the last you are to cook for him."

"But..."

"Jinny, I have spoken, and that be the end of it."

She bowed her head. The spoken word had never stopped her sister in the past, and she doubted it would now. However, Glendon was her husband, and he meant well. Yet, he could not know or even guess the fury his words would bring down on the wife he seemed to care about. Obeying him was not the problem – caring for Owena without him finding out, was.

CHAPTER 12

BY THE TIME JINNY WOKE up the next morning, Glendon was already gone. The sun was coming up, and when she looked outside, it promised to be another pleasant spring day. She quickly dressed and slipped out before her sister woke up. This time, thankfully, Owena was not throwing things, and Kam would let her sleep in. She hurried down the hill and was soon greeted by the dog and three puppies. Jinny giggled, sat down in the tall grass and played with all four. It was indeed a glorious way to start the day.

She was happy. It would not last, but for now, she was happy.

When she looked, Ronson and Mayzie were arm-in-arm atop of the hill as usual watching her. As soon as she could without a dog in her arms, she waved to let them know she was not still ill. The MacGreagors were beginning their day too, most just as happy as she to know that Owena was not out and about – or so Jinny assumed.

Several of the men had the deer carcasses hung from the limb of a tree and were carefully skinning each so as to keep from cutting holes in the fur. The meat had arrived just in time, and the hides would keep someone warm come winter, perhaps even her. Kam, she noticed was one of them. Odd how she hadn't the time to think of him much, but she did wonder how it would be if the wives were reversed. Would she have been happy being Kam's wife? Perhaps. However, she was starting to like Glendon, and would not wish her sister on him. The truth be told, she would not wish Owena on any man, not even Kam.

Just as Bradana had, when she spotted Cerdic watching her, she waved. Instantly his eyes grew large, and then he hurried off. Jinny laughed.

Having her fill of the dogs, she shooed them away, got up and decided to gather wildflowers for her table. There was just something about flowers that brightened a day, even hers. She thought to gather enough for Owena too, but when she looked, Glendon had joined his parents on the hill and he too was watching her. Everyone it seemed was watching her, and keeping Owena happy this day was not going to be easy, not now that they were giving her husband a full report of Jinny's activities.

HIS MOTHER WENT TO begin her day of work, leaving Glendon and his father alone standing on the hill. Glendon watched his wife gather flowers for a time, and then sighed. "She seems happy this mornin'."

"Aye." Ronson said. "Yesterday, she spoke to no one but her sister, not even your mother, though Mayzie dinna approach her. No one did."

"Do you suppose she thinks we shun her?"

"Nay, she was upset. I think to have a talk with her. Do you object?"

"Not at all. 'Tis time for you to get to know her better." Glendon suddenly chuckled. "She wishes to become a hunter so she may be without her sister for a whole day."

Ronson raised an eyebrow. "I can see why. Has she accepted you?"

"Not yet, but I can wait."

"Then you are wise. I waited for your mother and never have I regretted it. Perhaps I shall take Jinny for a ride to the mountains."

"If she will allow it. She frets that Owena shall constantly plague us if she is not here."

"And Jinny thinks 'tis hers to prevent it? Owena is Kam's wife, and 'tis his to see that she does not plague us."

"How?" Glendon asked. "Jinny knows of no way to prevent her shouting."

"A way shall come, and hopefully sooner rather than later."

MORE THAN THE MACGREAGORS were watching Jinny. Deep in the woods, Ian Battie peeked out from behind a tree and was pleased to find Jinny away from Owena's cottage. Now all he had to do was wait for Owena to come out, so he could whisk her away on his horse before the MacGreagors could catch him. He had it all planned, and even had a cloth with which to bind her mouth so Owena could not cry out.

He had been there to spy on her the day before too, but her pesky sister seemed always to be near, and when Owena finally did come out, her sister was with her. Furthermore, it had not been easy for Ian to stay out of sight as he followed them to the Lennox village. Twice, he had to go deeper into the forest, and cross over a hill, just to keep up. No sooner had he arrived than Owena and her sister turned right around and went back. Frustrated, Ian gave up and headed home.

Now he was back, it was early, Kam had gone into the village, her sister was a considerable distance away, and all he needed to do was wait for Owena.

WHILE SHE WAS PICKING flowers, and while her sister still slept, Jinny decided to gather some longer heather stems for her basket. Providing Owena did not take up too much of her time, or provoke her to distraction, she might actually come close to finishing her first MacGregor basket. That would please her very much, for there was little she found more satisfying than the feeling of accomplishment.

She was surprised then, when Laird MacGreagor and Glendon came toward her, each riding a magnificent black and white horse. That was something else she loved – dogs and horses.

Glendon swung down, and then held his hand out to her. "Father wishes to show you the glen."

Instantly alarmed, she stared at her husband, "I dare not go. Owena shall..."

With his hand still held out to her, he said, "He is your laird. You cannae deny him."

Jinny looked at Ronson's nod, back at Glendon, and then at the cottages. After taking a deep breath, and then slumping, she finally agreed. Glendon took her hand, turned her around, lifted her up and sat her on his horse. As soon as she was situated, he handed her the reins. "Are you not comin'?"

"I cannae, I've work to do."

"As do I," she argued.

He grinned, "Sadly, he is my laird too and like you, I must obey him."

"Come, Jinny," said Ronson. "I've a waterfall I should like you to see." When he turned his horse down the path that ran alongside the loch, she followed him.

Even so, she looked back, not once but several times. Owena would not be pleased to find her gone, and she would likely pay for it later. Then again, perhaps they might be back before her sister woke up. After all, Ronson had work of his own to do, or so she hoped.

It took time for her to relax, but she had to admit the breeze in her face, the smell of the forest, and the chirping of the birds brightened her mood. Glendon's horse seemed as gentle as her husband, and was easy to manage. Her laird had not yet spoken and she wondered why. Hopefully, he too would not be asking how to manage her sister. Jinny was flat out of answers to that question.

At length, Ronson said, "My son chose well for himself."

"Which son?" Jinny could not help but tease.

Ronson chuckled. "The one you married."

She lightly bit her lip, but she said it anyway, "I was not his first choice."

"First matters not, choosing well matters most."

She considered explaining that she was not exactly chosen, but decided to let him believe what he wished. "Shall we not go back now?"

He frowned and turned to her. "Before we see the waterfall?"

"How much further must we go?"

Ronson pulled his horse to a halt, which caused her horse to stop also. "Jinny, if you are in anguish, we shall go back now. Glendon said you desire to have time away from your sister's demands."

"I..."

"Did you not ask to be a hunter?"

Jinny finally smiled, "I believe I did."

"Then here you are, a hunter if you like, with time away from your sister. Perhaps you might see it as a kindness from me to you, and take it as such."

He was right. She had been so consumed with her worries, she neglected to realize her new laird was trying to grant her wish. She hung her head. "I fear you think me foolish."

"Nay, I think you trapped in a place you dinna choose, and with people you dinna seek. I might feel the same given your circumstance."

She found his remark puzzling, for she could not at first guess how he knew. Surely Glendon had not spoken of the way her being there came about. Yet, somehow Ronson did know. Perhaps William told him, or perhaps she had not paid particular attention to Glendon as any other happy wife would have. Whatever the reason, he was right. "Have you a remedy for feeling trapped?"

"I can offer only this – you may seek your comfort with me and my wife, day or night as the need may be."

"When Glendon is away?"

"Aye, and when he is home too. Life is not easy for a new wife. Our ways are different, and our work is hard, but we think ourselves happy. In time, we pray you shall be happy too."

That was not likely, but Jinny did not say so.

"What say you? Shall we not see the waterfall then? 'Tis not that much farther."

This time her smile was genuine. Ronson was kind, and if Glendon was as much like his father as he seemed to be, perhaps she would find some measure of true happiness after all.

THE MORNING PEACE IN the MacGreagor glen did not last long.

Owena was awake! Twice she screamed for Jinny before she harshly shoved her door open, making it loudly bang against the outside wall of her cottage. Several people stopped in their tracks for a time and then moved on.

Skinning a deer, Kam heard her and ignored her.

Glendon ignored her too. He promised to dig a fire pit for his wife, and hoped to have it done before she came back, but soon decided against finding himself that close to Owena. Instead, he went to the edge of the loch to wash the dirt off his hands.

"KAM!" Owena shouted. "JINNY!" When neither answered or came to her aid, she cupped her hands and shouted again, as if the shape of the glen did not already magnify her voice.

Joining her brother at the water, Bradana stifled a giggle with her hand. "Perhaps she might lose her voice."

"If she keeps that up, she surely will," said Glendon.

She washed her hands too, walked behind her brother, and then dried her hands on the back of his shirt. The cold water made him wiggle and made her laugh. "I helped Jinny with her wash yesterday."

"I thought it must be you. I thank you for that. She was so tired she was asleep when I got home." Glendon knelt down, dipped his hands in the water and twice washed his face. He had just gotten to his feet and was wiping his face on his sleeve, when Owena tapped him on the shoulder. Surprised, he quickly turned around.

"Where is she?" Owena demanded.

"Gone," he answered. He put his hands on his sister's shoulders, turned her around, and started the two of them walking toward the middle of the village.

Owena's voice began to rise. "Gone where? She is well aware I need her, and..."

He stopped and turned around to face Jinny's sister. "Need her for what?"

"She is to take care of me!"

"Why?"

"Because I am to be the next MacGreagor mistress. 'Tis her duty."

Glendon found her admission somewhat shocking. It certainly explained why Owena was so pleased to marry Kam, and he should have guessed that before. "I see. Yet, Jinny is my wife. She is to care for me and then you, if she has time. I expect she shall have little time for you, now that she is making baskets."

"You are mistaken, Jinny has always had time for me, and to make baskets besides."

"Not anymore."

"Dare you deny me? I shall have a word with my husband if you do."

"Very well." Glendon stretched out his arm and pointed. "Kam is that way."

Owena huffed, whipped past Glendon, and headed for her husband. Before Glendon could catch her, Bradana hurried off after Owena, giggling the whole way. He too followed, curious to see how well his brother would handle his wife. Future laird or not, Kam's stern abilities were about to be tested.

As he walked behind Owena and Bradana, Glendon noticed others were walking that way too. In particular, his aunt, Rossalyn, was coming from the other direction and she carried with her a flat pan and a stick. He could not imagine what she was up to, but he suspected whatever it was, it had to do with Owena.

When she approached and her husband had still not acknowledged her, Owena screamed, "KAM!" Kam turned around just in time to see Rossalyn come up behind his wife. She lifted the pan up next to Owena's ear, and then use the stick to begin beating on it.

Owena instantly spun around, narrowed her eyes, and yelled, "DARE YOU FRIGHTEN ME?"

Rossalyn raised her voice as well. "DARE YOU CONSTANTLY SCREAM?" Instead of backing off when she saw Owena's fierce glare, Rossalyn returned with one of her own, and banged the pan twice more.

Glendon was about to get between the two women when Kam gave his command.

"Owena, go home!" Kam said in a calm, collected tone of voice.

Thankfully, she lowered her voice as well, though she remained defiant. "I shall not go home! I wish to know where my sister is, and Glendon..."

Kam stuck his face right in hers and gritted his teeth, "I command you to go home, and go now!"

Just as Jinny predicted, not even that intimidated Owena. Instead, she casually glanced at all the people watching to see what she would do next. Most of them looked angry, and worse, Rossalyn was holding up her pan threatening to beat on it again. Owena shrugged and turned back to face her husband. "I only wish to know..."

"Wife, if you dinna obey me, I shall throw you in the loch."

Her eyes widened. "But, I cannae swim."

"Then you best go home!"

She looked into his determined eyes, glanced around once more at all the resentful faces, and then took a step toward her cottage. "I find I am too tired to abide such nonsense as this just now." She was certainly in no hurry as she walked away, but she did go home.

The moment Owena closed her cottage door, she heard the people begin to cheer and applaud. In a huff, she plopped down on the bed and angrily stared at the floor in front of her. "How dare they treat me thusly so?" Her eyes soon exposed not her anger but her fury. "Jinny has done this to me. No doubt she asked to be taken away...to where, I dinna know, but away from her duties to me. Indeed, 'tis all Jinny's fault."

CHAPTER 13

GLENDON WAS GLAD TO see a smile on Jinny's face when she and his father came back to the village. He went to her, reached up and then pulled her off his horse. He handed the reins to his father and then waited while Ronson took the horses away. As he began to walk beside her toward their cottage, he asked, "What say you of the waterfall?"

"Never have I seen such beauty."

"Then we shall go often. 'Tis best in spring, and in summer..."

Jinny looked everywhere but did not see her sister. "Is Owena not yet awake."

"Aye, she is awake and shouting, but Kam sent her home."

Jinny stopped walking and widened her eyes. "Sent her home?"

"Aye, she was..."

"She is upset then?"

"Likely, but Jinny all is well. I said you have not the time to tend to her now that..."

Jinny did not stay long enough to hear the rest of his sentence. Instead, she lifted the front of her skirt and started to run toward the incline.

"Jinny, what is it?" he called after her. He thought to run too, but decided just to let her go.

She did not, alas could not, stop to talk for she feared what was to come and she was right. Before Jinny could make it halfway up the incline, Owena stepped out from behind a tree and got directly in her sister's path.

With all her might, Owena slapped Jinny hard across the face. "DINNA EVER LEAVE ME AGAIN!"

The force of Owena's slap was so great as to knock Jinny backward and to the ground.

Dismayed, Glendon started to run. At the same time, he yelled, "KAM, OWENA HURT JINNY!" Afraid Owena would hit her again, he rushed to get between his wife and her sister. "Stand back, Owena," he ordered.

She fluttered her eyes as if what had just happened was of no consequence whatsoever, but she did move away. It was then he turned around to check on his wife. Jinny's nose was bleeding and her cheek was bright red, but thankfully, she was not knocked out. He knelt down, helped her sit up, took a rag out of his pocket, and helped her hold it to her nose. He kept his hand on her back in case she passed out, and then turned to glare at Owena.

It seemed like forever, but it was less than a moment before Kam came running up the incline. He was soon followed by his mother and sister. Both instantly went to tend to Jinny's injuries. Still glaring at his wife's attacker, Glendon stood back up. He knew better than to physically threaten her, but the expression on his face let it be known he wanted to.

Kam took one look at Jinny's injuries and grabbed hold of Owena's arm. "What have you done?"

"She is bad-mannered and deserved it," Owena whined.

By then, half the clan had gathered at the bottom of the incline.

Kam let go of Owena's arm and quickly grabbed both of her shoulders. "'Tis forbidden to hurt a lass or a child out of anger. 'Tis death to do it!"

"Death?" she gasped.

"Perhaps you dinna yet know our ways, but you shall."

Owena tried to wiggle out of his grasp, "I care nothing for your ways."

"So you have said. Nevertheless, a punishment be on you. You must never hurt your sister again!"

"What punishment?" Owena did not have time to hear his answer before her husband tackled her around the waist, and once more threw her over his shoulder. This time she did not think it was funny, and instead began screaming and beating his back with her fists. She did not seem to notice everyone laughing at her, as they parted to let Kam through, and then followed him past the edge of the village to the loch.

As soon as Mayzie and Bradana helped Jinny get up, she took the bloody rag away from her nose. "She cannae swim and she shall surely drown."

"Fret not," Mayzie assured her. "My son shall not harm her."

"He only means to get her wet," Glendon said. He hoped to get Jinny inside, but his wife was unable to take her eyes off her sister. At least her nose had stopped bleeding. Together, the four of them watched as Kam waded into the water, pulled is wife off him and tossed her in. The second she emerged, he reached for her, lifted her into his arms, and carried her back out of the water.

Amid the laughter and cheers, Jinny released a loud sigh.

"Come," said Glendon. "You must see to your rest."

"There now, 'tis over and done with," Mayzie said.

Jinny suddenly burst into tears. "'Tis never over and done with."

Glendon opened the door for her, helped her sit on the bed, and then knelt down in front of her. "Jinny, has she hurt you before?"

She was reluctant. He was her husband and Jinny was obliged to tell him the truth. Yet, his mother and sister were there, so she continued to hesitate. She watched Mayzie wet another clean cloth in the water bucket and bring it too her. Jinny put it against her swelling cheek bone and closed her eyes.

"'Tis good to tell us," Glendon urged. "We are your family now."

She could not keep the tears from rolling down her cheeks. Instead of saying it out loud, she slowly raised the sleeve on her left arm, and showed him a hideous burn scar. There were other scars too – deep fingernail scratches, bites, and cuts, she often lied about to protect her sister.

Glendon was so taken aback, he stood up and shook his head. "So this is what frightens you so?"

At last, Jinny managed to get control of her emotions. Finally admitting the truth of her sister's cruelty seemed to lift the heavy burden off her shoulders. She used the cloth to wipe her tears away, tried to smile, and then nodded. Her new found freedom did not last long.

Suddenly, the door of the next door cottage slammed shut. Owena was back and she was not happy. Jinny jumped, Bradana hurried out to see the excitement for herself, and Mayzie put a hand on Jinny's arm to comfort her.

Glendon gave his wife his solemn pledge, "She shall not hurt you again. I will not let her."

Just then, someone knocked on their door. Kam abruptly opened it and stuck his head in. "I fear throwing her in the loch has done little good. She is more upset now than before."

"I must go to her," Jinny muttered.

"Indeed not," Glendon said. "It does no good to let her have her way."

"You cannae protect me always and I alone can calm her. Owena regrets hurting me. She always regrets it."

"Aye, but..." Glendon started to argue. When his mother shook her head, he relented and followed his brother out. Before he closed the door, he looked back at his wife. "'Tis my honor to protect you. Dinna deny me that."

Outside, both Kam and Glendon watched as Owena again shoved open her door. One item at a time, she began to throw her wet clothes out.

"I am not inclined to pick them up," said Kam.

"Nor am I," Glendon agreed. He went to the log they sat on together while building their cottages, and thought to mention how they argued over who would marry Owena. Yet, he felt bad enough for his brother and bringing it up would be unkind.

Soon, Kam joined him, picked up a small stone, examined the shape of it, and then tossed it away. He started to say something, changed his mind, and then started again, "Perhaps we might take the rest of her clothes away."

"Aye, but she finds no shame in coming outside in her under things."

"True, but surely, if she were naked..."

"Yet we must leave her a blanket to keep her warm at night, and she shall always have need to leave the cottage occasionally."

Kam thoughtfully looked away. "Father would not let us imprison her anyway."

"True."

"What then?"

"I know not. Jinny says her father did everything he could to tame Owena."

"There must be something – there is always..." Before he could finish his sentence, Owena came to the door. She was fully dressed, and did not bother to close her door to keep the flies out when she started down the incline. He almost laughed when her shoes squished, but he contained himself. Instead, Kam just watched her go. In a little while, he stood up and began to follow. "I suppose I best see where she goes."

GLENDON'S MOTHER WAS just coming out when he started for the door. Mayzie said, "She is resting. Stay with her while I calm your father, for he has surely heard by now,"

"Owena just left and Kam is following her. We know not to where she goes."

"Good," his sister sighed. "Now we can all be calm."

"Have you no chores?" her mother asked.

"Oh that," Bradana frowned. "But first, I shall bring a puppy to Jinny. She loves the puppies."

"Very well, be off with you then." Mayzie turned back and gave her son a quick hug. "Jinny is a good lass, though she needs more kindness than most."

He watched her leave, and then went inside. Laying on the bed, Jinny opened her eyes for a moment to see who it was, and then closed them again. "Owena is gone," he whispered.

"I know, I heard you and Kam talking."

When she started to get up, he took her arm and helped her. "You should rest."

"Aye, but if I am up, the others shall not fuss over me so."

"That wife, you shall have to get used to." When she sat at the table, so did he. "You should see how they fuss when I so little as have a splinter in my hand." He hoped to and was glad when he made her smile. Her cheek was turning a light shade of blue, but it was not as bad as he imagined it would be.

"I have not yet fetched food for our supper."

"Well, you have hardly had a chance to. I can..."

"Nay, *I* can. Let them see that I dinna suffer as much as some may say."

"Very well, then I shall go with you." She was standing up, had grabbed the empty pot, and was out the door before he managed to get up. It made him smile.

"I am glad of one thing this day," she said as they walked together down the incline. "I am glad Kam dinna choose me to be his mistress, for I have always hated being the daughter of a Laird. Father never had enough time for mother or for us. He was always off seeing to one problem or another. Owena resented it far more than I, but I confess I often wished for a long walk with him in the woods, or even a meal on a blanket in a meadow. It was not to be." If she noticed that Glendon had no comment to make on the subject, she paid little attention. Instead, she waved and smiled at everyone she saw, just to relieve their worried expressions.

Everything had gone back to normal – just as it always did after one of Owena's fits of rage.

IAN BATTIE ARRIVED just in time to watch Owena make her way across the stonewall and walk toward the Lennox village. He'd been thinking about Teva MacGreagor, the woman he dearly loved all morning, and almost decided to watch her instead. However, the only way to get Laird MacGreagor to let him marry Teva was to have something to barter, and taking Kam's wife and then offering to bring her back in exchange was the perfect idea. After seeing the sisters visit the Lennox the day before, he hoped they would be back, and finding Owena alone was even better.

He tied his horse to a tree, and then slipped through the bushes to get a better look. She was not even half way to the village when one of the Lennox warriors walked up to her. Although he could not hear what was said, it was not hard to guess what the two of them had in mind.

Suddenly, Kam MacGreagor shouted. "OWENA, COME BACK HERE!"

As quickly as he could, Ian crouched down even lower, making certain not to be seen. With two fingers, he carefully parted the bushes just in time to watch Kam's wife turn and face her husband. At the same time, the man she thought to meet quickly spun around and ran off.

Owena screamed, "DARE YOU COMMAND ME AFTER WHAT YOU HAVE DONE?"

Kam stood on the other side of the wall with his hands on his hips. "DINNA MAKE ME COME AFTER YOU!"

Owena looked back, notice the Lennox was gone, and shrugged. She lifted the front of her skirt, took a slow exaggerated step toward her husband, and then another.

Thoroughly disgusted, Kam turned around and walked away.

Now was his chance. Ian waited until she slowly came even with his hiding place and then stood up. He softly whistled to get her attention, and waved her over. Owena pondered the invitation, but just for a moment before she headed his direction.

"I know you," she said, you are from Clan Battie.

"Aye, I am Ian. Shall you not take a ride with me?"

She giggled and emphatically nodded. Soon, she made her way through the bushes, squishy shoes and all, and when he took her to his horse, she let him lift her up, untie the reins, and then mounted behind her.

He had her at last, and with very little effort on his part. Not long after, she began to tell him all about her miserable life as the wife of Kam MacGreagor. He simply nodded, appropriately commented when necessary, and took his captive back to the road and turned toward his home.

CERDIC HAD BEEN DOING a little spying of his own. He secretly had an eye for Bradana now that he'd gotten over the age of finding lasses repulsive. She seemed to like him too, although he was never quite certain if she fancied him or liked taunting him. Nevertheless, he found himself an eyewitness to the most exciting thing that had happened in his entire lifetime – the escape, or at least he thought it was an escape, of Kam MacGreagor's wife.

"OWENA IS GONE!" AN excited Bradana said as soon as she found her brother. He was obviously upset, for he was walking fast and his fists were clenched. She held a puppy in her arms, and was nearly out of breath. Kam seemed not to hear her, so she quickened her step in an attempt to keep up with him. "Did you not hear me?"

"Aye, I heard it well enough. She shall come back."

"Nay, she rode off with a Battie. 'Tis the same Battie what asked to marry Teva."

Kam abruptly stopped walking and turned to look at her. "Truly? You saw her?"

"Aye. I wished to see what she would do and was watching when she went into the bushes with him. She got on his horse willingly."

At first, Kam did not seem to know whether to go forward, go back, or go for his horse. In the end, he just stood there and looked around. "I shall see to it. Go tell Jinny, she shall want to know. The last I saw of her, Jinny was near one of the cellars."

Bradana did not have to be told twice, and hurried off to find her sister-in-law.

He watched as his little sister got to the cellar just as Jinny was coming out. Just then, he spotted his father walking down a village path and hurried after him. "Father, Owena is gone," he said when he caught up.

Ronson quickly turned around. "Gone where?"

"Bradana saw her ride away with Ian Battie."

Ronson stared at the ground for a moment. There were others nearby, so he kept his voice to just above a whisper. "I care not to go to war with the Battie."

"Nor do I, but 'tis the honorable thing to do. She is my wife."

"Aye, she is that right enough." Ronson glanced around, and then turned his back to a man who seemed unusually interested in the conversation. The man took the hint and went about his business. "Perhaps Ian shall soon know his mistake and bring her back."

"We wait then?"

"Aye, we wait."

Although Ronson and Kam did not mean for word to spread throughout the clan, Bradana had other ideas. Not often had she seen such excitement, and she wasn't about to let the saga of a wayward bride go unnoticed. Soon, everyone was talking, and then asking what Kam intended to do about it. Flustered and soon angry that Owena had gone willingly, Kam simply said, "We wait to see if the Battie bring her back."

That caused even more speculation. Some of the men took to sharpening their weapons while the women saw to making extra flat cakes and hauling more water. After years of peace with hardly even a minor skirmish, their hearts were racing and their minds spinning.

THEY KNEW IT NOT, BUT there was about to be an uproar in the Battie village.

With a grin on his face, Ian Battie walked his horse down the paths between the many cottages and up to the laird's house. He dismounted, and then helped Owena down. That the people stared was not unexpected, for she was indeed bonnie, and soon they began to gather around. While Owena was busy smoothing the wrinkles of her skirt, the massive double doors of the laird's house swung open.

Laird Battie, a hearty man with a receding hairline, looked admiringly at Owena and was pleased when she finally noticed him and smiled. "Who might you be?" he asked.

"I am Kam MacGreagor's wife."

Laird Battie's brows shot up, his eyes widened, and his mouth dropped. "A MacGreagor? Is your husband not with you?"

Ian boldly stepped forward. "I have taken her."

"Taken her? What mean you, lad?"

"He means my husband knows not where I am, nor does he care. Just this morning, Kam carried me off and threw me in the loch. I have come seeking refuge, for I no longer wish to be his wife."

As if it were possible, Laird Battie's eyes widened even more. "Refuge? We cannae give refuge to the wife of a MacGreagor."

Owena narrowed her gaze. "I say you can, and you shall!" She caused quite a stir among the people, but she did not care.

"What?"

A confused Ian looked from his laird to Owena and back again. "Nay, 'tis not how 'tis to be. I mean to give her back once Laird MacGreagor says I may marry Teva. I mean only to..."

Owena raised her voice. "I shall not go back!"

In return, Laird Battie stiffened his resolve. "You shall do as I say!"

This time, Owena's voice raised a complete octave and screamed, "NAY, I SHALL NOT!"

Astounded by her insolence, Laird Battie scratched the side of his beard.

Rarely had anyone stood up to their laird, particularly not a woman. The stir among the people became a rumbling and then they raised voices of their own. "SHE IS CURSED!" one shouted. "AND SHE BRINGS THE CURSE TO US!" yelled another.

The laird's wife tugged on his sleeve to get his attention. "Will the MacGreagors attack us?"

That was something he had not yet considered. He took a careful look around, first at the large size of his village, at the livestock grazing in the pastures, the people, and then at the children. They constantly stayed ready for an attack from the MacKellar, but those were always small battles and never full out wars. He was well aware the Battie were smaller men, and any idea of intentionally fighting MacGreagors was ridiculous. Still, he would attack any clan that took his wife, even the MacGreagors, for it was the honorable thing to do.

Fully alarmed, he shouted, "LADS, ARM YOURSELVES!"

In all haste, the people in the Battie village began scurrying this way and that. The men put on their full armor, as much as they had, and took up positions facing the road from which the MacGreagors would surely come. Terrified women did just as the MacGreagor women were doing – making extra food, rounding up their children, and carrying extra water in case of cottage fires. They were prepared, if necessary, to hide in the forest if a battle should begin. Indeed, they were quite used to that.

"Ian, take her to your cottage," Laird Battie ordered.

"Nay," Owena argued, "I am to be the next MacGreagor mistress, and I must stay in the laird's house. What shall my husband say if he finds me in lesser lodgings?"

"She is right," Laird Battie muttered. "Very well then, you shall stay here." He barely had time to get out of the way before Owena whipped past him, and disappeared inside.

To Owena, the place looked more like the castles she had heard about than the usual laird's house. In the great hall, there were colorful wall hangings, candles in holders, and a long table with actual chairs down the center of the room. "A bench, indeed," she mumbled.

Behind her, Mistress Battie watched her guest with interest. It was not until Owena turned around and began to speak that she raised an eyebrow.

"I shall have chicken for my supper, and a mug of your best drink." Owena did not wait for an answer, before she turned back around and continued to visually inspect the place. "How many servants have you?"

"Servants? We have no servants."

"Helpers then?"

"Nay, no helpers. I tend to the keeping of this house myself."

The Battie hearth was made of very fine red rock and larger than any she had ever seen. A supper pot had not yet been hung over the fire, but it was still early. "Well, when I am mistress, I shall have a very fine house, much finer than this, with many servants to tend my needs."

"You mean to go home then?"

"Aye, someday when they sufficiently regret having lost me."

Mistress Battie finally walked across the room to the hearth, and then used a stick to stir the embers. "Your supper shall be the same as ours. We are having mutton, and you shall also drink what best suits us."

Owena's ire swiftly rose and likewise the volume of her voice, "I DEMAND CHICKEN, OR I SHALL SAY YOU NEGLECTED TO FEED ME!"

Shocked, Mistress Battie dropped the stick, carefully skirted her way around her insolent guest, and fled out the door. She ran this way and then that until she discovered her husband's location. Nearly out of breath, she recounted the conversation. "I'll not feed her. I'll not have such as her in my house!"

"Wife," said he, trying to approach the situation sensibly, "what am I to do with her?"

"I care not what you do, but she shall not stay in my house!" She huffed, stomped off, and then mumbled, "Chicken, indeed! We've not had chicken ourselves in months."

Her husband had more than enough to worry about as it was. He was so troubled, that he demanded Ian go to the front of the line of defense so he would be the first to die. Ian tried desperately to say that was not how he intended it to be, but Laird Battie listened not and fiercely glared until Ian obeyed.

While they stood at the ready to fight, the men were talking among themselves and each of them had the same question. If they should kill a MacGreagor, men with a curse upon them, would the curse pass to the Battie? He did not know. How could he? A more pressing question was this – would his men be in such fear of the curse as to refuse to fight? Laird Battie could not hide the overwhelming distress in his expression.

It could mean the end of him, alas, it could mean the end of all of them.

UNFORTUNATELY FOR THE Battie, Owena had just begun to make her demands. She screamed for someone to dry her shoes and wash her feet. Next, she wanted her hair brushed, the fire stoked, and something to eat, for she had neglected to take her noon meal. When she was told the Battie need the eggs and that chicken was out of the question, she decided duck would do. When Mistress Battie shook her head, Owena screamed, "DUCK, I SHALL HAVE DUCK, AND YOU SHALL GIVE IT TO ME!"

IN THE MACGREAGOR VILLAGE, an hour passed and then two and still Owena had not returned. The glen had become peaceful once more, and everyone was relieved save Jinny. She tried to concentrate on preparing a noon meal and them setting supper over the embers to cook, but every thought she had was about her sister.

When she went to get more water from the loch, she paused to look at her reflection. Her face had stopped hurting, although it was still sensitive when she touched it. She dipped her hands in the water, splashed it on her face, and then carefully blotted the wetness away with the hem of her skirt. She was not surprised when Glendon picked up the bucket and again filled it for her.

"As you can see, I am quite well," she assured him.

"Aye, but are you not upset still?"

"I fear for my sister, if that is what you mean. She is...I mean, the way she is cannae be looked upon kindly by those who know not how to comfort her."

"She is Kam's wife. They shall not harm her, and as soon as they see the way she is they shall surely bring her back."

At last, Jinny grinned. "Aye, they shall. I see that now." She reached down and picked up the bucket. "Have you naught to do?" He winked and then walked away.

After that, she went home and tried working on her basket, but too often, she instead stood in front of the window watching for her sister. She was not quite convinced the Battie would not harm her, for she had seen the rage in many an eye where her sister's belligerence was concerned. Many a man, and a woman, was tempted to do Owena in.

Yet, the time continued to pass, the sun moved across the sky, the MacGreagors carried on as usual, and still Owena was not back. So very often, Jinny wished for just that sort of solitude, and should be enjoying it, but she feared never seeing her sister again.

Some days with Owena were not that bad, and in spite of her sister's occasional cruelty, Jinny loved her. She just never found a way of convincing Owena that life would be far happier if she would consider others instead of herself only.

That night, Jinny served her husband his dinner without saying a word. Instead of eating, she separated her onions from the other vegetables, and then mixed them together again.

"Are you not hungry?"

"Why does Kam not go after her?"

"Father fears chasing after her could start a war. There is word among the Lennox, that she is yet unharmed."

"Oh."

"Shall the lads go after her tomorrow?"

Glendon answered, "I know not, 'tis up to Father."

"And not Kam?"

"Aye, and Kam as well."

She once more thoughtfully stirred the food in her bowl. "I think of the day he married her often. I knew 'twas a mistake, but said nothing."

"Because he deserved it for not choosing you?"

"Partly, but 'twas a far more selfish reason. I dreamed of a life without her, and dinna think..."

"You would end up married to me and living in the same village."

She closed her eyes for a moment and then opened them again. "Aye, but I see now she would have found a way for us to live together, be it with the MacGreagors or another clan. We might even have been forced to remain with the Allaway, though I cannae imagine Father would have allowed that in the end. So you see, it was to be, and there was no way of avoiding it. Only..."

"Only what?"

"Only the MacGreagors have such goodness in their ways, I wish, I truly wish I had somehow prevented Kam from marrying her."

"Kam had his heart set. He would not have listened even if you had warned him."

"Truly?"

"Truly. My brother and your sister are more alike than you know. You shall see that too someday." He finished his last bite and then pushed his bowl out of the way. "The lads shall be coming back soon. They took the last of the barter to trade for spices. Mother says we are in need of nearly everything, and we hoped to have enough salt to cure the meat again this year. What spice do you favor most?"

She giggled, "All of them."

"As do I."

The sun was down by the time they finished their meal, and once more Glendon slept on the floor and she in the bed. She was beginning to think of him as more than just a stranger. So far, if he was ill-tempered, he had not shown it. His father did not seem to be, nor his brother. She felt she should say something, and when she looked, the full moon shining through the window let her know his eyes were not closed.

"Glendon?"

"Aye."

"I no longer fancy your brother."

"Then we are even, for I no longer fancy your sister."

She giggled, turned over, and went to sleep.

CHAPTER 14

WHILE THE MACGREAGORS enjoyed a good slumber, the Battie did not.

Twice, they heard gray wolves in the forest howling in response to her shouts. Still concerned that the MacGreagor might attack at night, the men took turns sleeping where they were – on the hard ground at the end of the road from where the enemy would surely come. Wives and children fretted long into the night, and when it was at last, peaceful enough to rest, Owena's latest demand woke them back up.

The last thing they heard from her was "TAKE ME HOME! I WISH TO BE WITH MY SISTER!"

No longer amazed that the MacGreagors had not come for her, for there was not a soul among them who did not understand why, not one but all of the Battie were eager to do just that – take her home. As the sun rose, those with little sleep groaned, moaned and some even swore a particular curse on Owena. The question then was – who shall take her back? Most suggested Ian, for he had brought her. That pleased Ian. He still hoped he might make a trade.

After careful consideration, however, Laird Battie decided he best take her himself, for fear the MacGreagors needed to be calmed down. Many a life had been lost over a kidnapped wife, and he hoped to spare the Battie of just such an outcome. He chose six of his stoutest men plus

Ian to go with him, had the horses brought forward, and together they waited for Owena to come out.

Mistress Battie attempted to wake her three different times. Frustrated beyond measure, she finally carried a full cup of water into the room where her guest slept and threw it in Owena's face. She quickly hid the cup, and then sweetly smiled. "My, how I shall miss your good company once you are gone."

Owena abruptly sat up, grabbed the corner of the blanket under which she slept, and wiped the water off her face. Before she could form her usual glower, Mistress Battie scampered out of the room. "Your ride awaits, my queen," she heard the mistress sarcastically announce.

Even then, it took a while for Owena to drag herself out of bed and find her shoes. At last, she stumbled out the double front doors as though she had partaken of too much wine, and cared not if her clothing were straightened. "'Tis not yet the noon sun," she moaned. Instead of going to the waiting horse, she took off into the woods to take care of the particulars.

Already frustrated and with plenty of spring work to do themselves, each and every man rolled his eyes, yet they all agreed on one thing – let the MacGreagors have their curse back!

IT WAS A LITTLE AFTER the noon sun when Birk rode hard into the MacGreagor village to spread the news – the Battie were seen coming up the road and they were bringing Owena with them. The men looked to Ronson to see if they should arm themselves, but Ronson shook his head and started up the hill. At the top, he could see some distance off, and indeed there was a cloud of dust and it was headed his way. It was not a big cloud of dust, and thereby he rightly suspected the number of Battie to be small. Ronson sighed his relief.

Shortly thereafter, both Kam and Glendon climbed the hill to stand with their father. Jinny was outside their cottage working on her basket when the commotion began, and when she looked up the hill, Glendon motioned for her to come too. She soon set her basket making aside and hurried that direction.

As soon as Jinny arrived, Kam sneered at her, "The good sister has come to welcome the bad."

"She is not all bad," Jinny protested.

"You cannae prove it by me," he mocked.

Jinny had heard enough and turned to fully face Kam. "I can prove this – you saw with your eyes and not with a clear mind. Now, because you chose wrongly, you care not what becomes of her." She turned her accusing eyes away. "Some fine laird you shall be."

Kam looked from his unsympathetic father, to his annoyed brother, and then down at the ground. "You mistake me sister-in-law, I shall care, but not just yet."

Not another word was said.

Nearly all the members of the clan had gathered in the courtyard in front of the laird's house, by the time Ronson led the way down the hill. He stopped in front of his cottage, stood with his legs apart, and clasped his hands behind his back in an unthreatening manner. When the other men saw it, they too clasped their hand behind them.

As they cautiously approached, the Battie slowed their horses to a gentle walk. Owena was grinning as though fully enjoying all the attention. When they reached the edge of the courtyard, Laird Battie raised his hand to stop them. He dismounted, handed his reins to another, took hold of Owena's halter, and led her horse through the crowd.

Behind him, Ian looked all over for his lost love, and when he found her, he shouted, "I HAPPILY TRADE OWENA FOR TEVA!"

The crowd murmured, Laird Battie raised his hand to silence his disobedient hunter, and then looked apologetically at Ronson. "My laddie took Kam's wife, though he claims she went willingly."

"Aye, she did," Ronson said.

His great relief was in the way Laird Battie sighed. "We care not to go to war with you, therefore..."

"There be no need for war. Your lad took her; therefore, he shall be pleased to keep her."

The blood began to drain out of Laird Battie's face. "Keep her?"

"WHAT?" Owena shouted. She disregarded the moans her piercing voice caused among the people. "I AM KAM'S WIFE. YOU MUST TAKE ME BACK!"

Kam boldly stepped forward. "I dinna want her back either. She is slothful and unruly. Why would I want her back?"

"Aye," Laird Battie tried to argue, "but..."

"None of us want her," a man in the crowd shouted, and when he did, the others cheered.

Owena glanced all around until her eyes landed on her sister. "Jinny, tell them. They must take me back! I am to be the next MacGreagor mistress."

Before Jinny could respond, Kam interrupted, "Nay, you are not. I gave my birthright to my brother so that I might have you. Your sister is to become the next MacGreagor mistress and not you."

Owena gasped, and so did Jinny.

Standing next to his wife, a worried Glendon looked down at her. "'Tis true?" she asked.

"Aye, but we vowed never to speak it until..."

"Until after I passed?" Ronson interrupted.

Both Glendon and Kam bowed their heads. "Aye, Father," Glendon finally admitted.

"I see." Ronson brought his hands from the back of him and folded them in the front the way he always did. "Well, what is said, cannae be unsaid." He nodded to Laird Battie, "My son has spoken. He dinna want his wife back. Of course, he may not ever have another, but I cannae say I blame him."

"Nor I," Laird Battie admitted. "She be impossible, nay worse than impossible, she be cursed."

"I agree," Ronson said. "Therefore, you may do as you please with her. Good morn' to you then."

"There be no other way?" Laird Battie asked. When he received no reply, he started to turn her horse around.

Owena screamed, "JINNY, DINNA LET THEM TAKE ME!"

It was then that Jinny finally stepped forward, "And still you shout at me? Do you never learn?"

Owena looked as though she might actually cry real tears. "I dinna mean to."

Jinny was far from convinced. "Of course you mean to, you always mean to."

"Well, perhaps I do."

Just like Ronson, and to show her resolve, Jinny tightly folded her arms. "And you make me do your part in the chores, is that not so?"

"Not all of them."

"Aye, all of them!"

"Perhaps I do, but..."

"And when I refuse your demands, you hurt me, is that not also true?" Jinny ignored the women who gasped or covered their shocked mouths in the crowd.

"I dinna mean to hurt you."

Jinny huffed, turned around and started to walk away.

"Very well, 'tis true, I have hurt you, but I shall never do it again."

Jinny stopped and looked back. "I have heard those words before. I dinna believe you then and I dinna believe you now." She again started to leave.

An actual tear rolled down Owena's cheek. "Jinny, you are all I have. You are all I have ever had." She allowed herself a quick sob. "What must I say then?"

After taking another long breath, Jinny turned back to her husband. "Can a MacGreagor mistress ban a sister who will not obey?"

Glendon did not hesitate to emphatically nod. "I shall see to sending her away myself."

Just to make certain, Jinny looked at Ronson and then Mayzie. Both readily agreed.

"Good." Jinny had never done it, nor seen it done before, but she walked to the center of the courtyard and put her hands on her hips. "This is my command. Owena, you shall rise when the sun breaks the crest of the mountains, and not go to bed before the day be complete. You shall care for Kam the way our mother cares for our father, you shall not command anything of me, and you shall never again scream, unless harm is about to befall you."

Owena slipped off the horse, ran to her sister, and then abruptly stopped. Remembering herself, she knelt in front of Jinny. "I swear it. If you let me stay, I shall do all that you say."

Jinny was not finished and did not make a move to relieve her sister's distress. "Give me... nay, give all of us your pledge."

Owena got up, slowly turned around to face everyone in turn, and sniffed back her tears, "I give you my pledge, my true pledge. I shall never be a bother again." She only got a few nods, but it was the approval of her future mistress that she needed most.

"Very well," Jinny finally conceded, "you may begin by washing the clothing you threw out of your cottage yesterday."

So happy was she, Owena hurried through the crowd, and started up the incline to her cottage. With every eye watching, she picked up each item of mud stained clothing, and darted inside. When she came back out, she held up a bar of lye soap. Owena actually laughed as she ran back down the incline, past the edge of the village, and then to edge of the loch.

"I best show her to the easy place," Bradana, said. She gave Jinny a quick hug, and then she too was gone. Little by little, the people who were not too stunned to move, began to drift away.

Yet all was not finished. "Teva?" Ian Battie asked.

"Married," Ronson answered.

Ian was crushed, turned his horse around, and slowly left the village.

"I am most grateful," Laird Battie confessed. "If ever you should..."

Ronson wrinkled his brow. "Are you of a mind to take the most worthless mule in all the world with you?"

"The one I can hear braying of a quiet summer morn?" When Ronson nodded, Battie rolled his eyes, "Not *that* grateful." He quickly mounted the horse he brought Owena on, motioned to his men, and led them toward home.

At last, all was back to normal, at least the kind of normal the MacGreagors had not seen in a few days. The rest of the people went back to their chores until only Ronson's family members remained in the courtyard.

"'Tis quite a sight to be seen," Kam said, motioning toward his wife. He watched as Bradana took Owena's hand and pulled her farther down the path and then out of sight.

"True," Jinny admitted. "Finally, we have solved the problem of Owena."

"Hopefully," Glendon said. "Kam be right about one thing – I got the good wife, and just now I find great honor in being her husband."

Instead of being flattered, Jinny said, "Aye, but I have a question still. Must you truly be the laird and I the mistress?"

It was Ronson who answered the question. "Well, if my eldest son somehow finds his clear mind, as you rightly put it, perhaps Glendon shall consider relenting. No matter which becomes laird, when a wife does not desire it, he can choose another to take her part."

"Then I am relieved. I have long thought not having a caring father be the trouble with Owena. All she truly wanted was his time, and when he dinna give it, she sought ways of demanding it."

Ronson deeply wrinkled his brow and turned to his wife. "Do I not spend enough time with our daughters?"

Mayzie looped her arm through his and started to walk him down to the loch. "Have I not been saying that forever? Your mind could use a little clearing as well."

Ronson looked back at Kam, rolled his eyes, and then allowed his wife to drag him away.

Kam chuckled. "I believe I might take a bucket of fresh water to the cottage, now that I am not being commanded to do it." He playfully bowed to his brother, and then headed home to get the bucket.

"I BELIEVE I HAVE WORK to do as well," Jinny said. She had just started to turn when Glendon touched her arm.

"Will you not walk with me? There is much I am in need of saying."

"But..."

"The work can wait." He held out his hand to her.

Jinny looked at his open hand, looked into brown eyes she failed to notice before, smiled and finally put her hand in his.

There were plenty of eyes watching, as Glendon took his bride for a walk on the path that ran alongside the loch. It was the same path his father had taken her on, and somehow on this morning it looked even more beautiful than it had the day before. She drew in the fresh air, savored the smell of the sudden burst of wildflowers, and laughed when the dogs began to follow them. Moreover, her hand felt grand in his. Twice she looked at the side of his face, as if to see it for the first time. When did he become so handsome?

They had gone quite a distance, and for the first time she felt free to be away from her sister. She was free, free to smile, free to enjoy the life she had been given, and even free to sing if she so desired. It was then that she realized the music was not in her head, but it was coming from the village. The MacGreagors were free again too.

When Glendon looked down at her, she smiled up at him. "I..."

"Say nothing, Jinny." He stopped and turned to her, but still he did not let go of her hand. "Allow me..." He paused to consider what he precisely wanted to say. "I believe 'twas the first day, when you played with Old Shep and your laughter filled the glen, I began to favor you. I know not precisely why, but I know from that day to this, I found you to be more pleasing than any wife I could have hoped for."

So completely unaccustomed to being flattered, she tried to turn her face away.

Glendon put a finger under her chin and gently turned her face back to him. "I love you, Jinny MacGreagor."

"You love me?" she asked.

"I dinna think it possible myself at first, but there it is. Might you...'tis possible you might love me too someday?"

It certainly had not happened the way she dreamed it would, but the quickened beat of her heart was just as she imagined. He loved her, he carried her off to a new and exciting life, and he was more handsome than Kam could ever be.

Did she love him? "I find you very agreeable," she finally managed to say, "save for..."

A disturbed expression crossed his face, "For what?"

She tipped her head to the side and looked up at him through the corner of her eyes, "Save for you have not yet kissed me. How can I know of love until..."

Before she could finish, he had her in his arms. Her lips were on his, and she became so lost in his embrace, she knew not that he lifted her completely off the ground. She heard not the music, she knew not if the earth was spinning around her, or if it was only in her head, and it mattered not. She loved him and would until the day she died.

In the village, there were indeed many eyes watching them, and many lips smiling as they sang their song – for therein lay the next MacGreagor generation.

~the end~

VIKING VALOR

Book 8
(The Viking Series)

Sample Chapter

S It was forbidden, but Bradana MacGreagor could not seem to help herself. The man of her dreams was a Lennox, and Laird Lennox forbid all unions between the two clans, fervently believing that the MacGreagors were cursed. Rubbish, said the MacGreagors, but that did nothing to persuade the Lennox. Too soon, her destiny was taken completely out of her hands when word came that the king had called all able-bodied men to fight for Scotland.

CHAPTER 1

NICOL, THE SECOND SON of the clan's laird, would long suffer the decision he made to leave the village well before sunrise that morning. Hunting was vastly important, for winter had not been kind to their small clan. An illness wiped out nearly half of them and due to an uncommonly dry summer, the land grew little. He and the brothers, Murdock and Inek, were young, of good health and strength, and loved the thrill of the hunt. The day before had been a particularly sad day, for it was then that the clan buried Nicol's gravely ill father. Nicol's elder brother, Edan, was now laird and all was well – or so Nicol thought. Had he guessed otherwise, he would have stayed home.

Their small peaceful clan lived in the northeast of Scotland on a stretch of flat land not far from the River Tay. Their glen was surrounded by sparsely wooded hills, some high and some no larger than a knoll. Animal paths crisscrossed the land, affording them various ways to access their village, yet there was one well-traveled road, the width of a two-wheel cart, that offered an easy ride, continued on to the Straiton village and beyond.

For the most part, the clan worked, laughed, loved, and survived the same as all other clans. With Viking raids a thing of the past, and the English far enough away not to be a bother, they feared little – save an occasional dispute with the Straiton, their nearest neighbor.

It was a dry day, not unlike the many dry days before it, although the clamminess in the air was unusually high for autumn. As the sun rose, the men began to see to their comfort, taking off layers of clothing, and stuffing them in leather pouches. The lack of rain encouraged the wildlife to come down out of the mountains in search of water, making the hunt far more prosperous – or so they hoped. However, the wildlife seemed far more scarce than they expected. For a time, the men left their horses and walked through the forest with arrows loaded and bows at the ready, hoping to catch sight of a red deer, or even a rabbit.

Good fortune simply was not theirs that day. As well, the more they walked, the farther they traveled from their village.

At noon they whistled for their horses, found a brook and stopped to have a bountiful meal of bread, cheese and dried beef, happily devouring the last crumb. The lack of wind added to their discomfort and that afternoon yielded no better opportunities to secure meat. At last, the time came to head home. It was not the first time they were put upon to return empty handed, but this time the lack of food would disappoint the clan.

"Perhaps we should stay the night and hunt in the morning," Murdock suggested. Just eighteen months older than his brother Inek, Murdock kept his long, light brown hair tied with string at the back of his neck just as most men did. Except for Murdock's beard and mustache being fuller and longer, the brothers looked very much alike.

Nicol, the oldest of the three with light blond hair, seriously considered Murdock's suggestion. A red deer or two would keep him from being embarrassed in front of the other young men he hoped to impress. Yet they brought nothing more to eat, and he was just as fond of a full meal as anyone else. Therefore, as the sun began to sink lower and the color of the evening sky began to turn to dusk, they headed down the main road toward home.

It was when they reached the crest of a hill that they guessed something was amiss. Inek halted his horse and smelled the air, not once but twice to be certain. "Fire?" he fearfully breathed, for he was well aware that nothing was more dangerous than a fast moving fire across lands that had seen no rain.

"Aye, but where?" Nicol slowly surveyed what he could see of the land from his vantage point, even turning his horse all the way around. Alas, the direction from which the smoke came was not easily determined. He finally shrugged. "Keep an eye out, lads." He urged his horse onward at a steady pace, constantly glancing this way and that with a careful eye. Even so, he saw nothing to alarm him and the smell of smoke seemed no more.

They were about to ride their horses over the last hill when Nicol's sister rushed out of a clump of trees and ran directly into their path. All three men instantly halted their horses in an effort not run over her.

Nicol was about to chastise her carelessness; until he saw the look of horror on her face. "What be it?"

Cait grabbed hold of his leg and breathlessly demanded, "Delay not, for we must hide!"

He thought it nonsense and frowned. "Hide from what?"

"The Straiton take three captive."

Even though he thought such a thing unlikely, he leaned down, lifted his sister up and sat her on his horse in front of him. He nodded for Murdock to lead the way and followed, hoping once they were safely in hiding he could get to the bottom of what Cait was talking about. A few minutes later, Murdock found a place that he deemed good cover and stopped.

By then, Nicol had noticed how dirty his sister's clothing was. That was not like her at all. Cait was always the one who attempted to look her best for all occasions, even working in the fields. As well, she had dirt in her hair, smudges on her face, and lines down her cheeks where tears had washed the dirt away. He gently wrapped both of his arms around her and let her lean against him. "Why have the Straiton attacked us?"

"They dinna attack," she started to say.

"Then..." Inek tried to interrupt.

"Let her speak," Nicol cautioned.

"Laird Straiton came to see us. He was uncommonly friendly and wished Edan well now that he had become our laird." She paused to take a forgotten breath and to brush the hair off her face. "Laird Straiton offered him the king's own wine to drink in celebration. They drank and drank until Edan could hardly stand."

He was beginning to fear the answer to his question, but he asked it anyway, "Did Laird Straiton kill him?"

"Nay," Cait answered, "'Twas worse."

"What could be worse?" Murdock asked.

"They made a wager," she answered, turning her attention to Murdock. "'Twas thought to be a jest at first. Laird Straiton wagered his land against ours that he could ride their slowest mare and yet win a race against our fastest stallion."

"Oh noooo," Nicol moaned. He closed his eyes. "I took our fastest horse." He thoughtfully rubbed his forehead for a moment. "Say Edan dinna lose our land?"

Cait emphatically nodded. "Aye, he did. When the wine began to leave his mind and he saw what he had done," she paused to take another, even deeper breath, "Edan went daft, plunged a dagger into his heart and died." She could fight back her tears no longer, allowed herself to collapse against her brother and began to sob. At length, she gathered her strength and gratefully took the cloth Nicol handed her so she could wipe the tears off her cheeks.

Nicol cast-off his own emotions and waited until his little sister was in control again before he asked. "Did they burn the village?"

"Nay. Laird Straiton said we could stay as long as we continued to work the land, take only what we need, and give the rest to him. Otherwise, we are to leave, but where shall we go? We have no place other."

"He cannae do that, can he?" Inek asked.

Cait continued, "Three lads tried to fight, and were taken away. We know not what has become of them."

"Who?" Murdock insisted.

"Logan, Peyton and Hensen. Logan thought to burn green wood in the lookout hearth so you might see it and stay away, but the fire went out directly." She hung her head for a moment. "When Cairn Straiton thought to marry me, Father denied him, but father be gone and... Nicol, I dinna want to marry Cairn Straiton. He be by far the most disagreeable unsightly lad I ever did see."

In spite of his upset, Nicol couldn't help but smile at her description of Cairn. He did not care for the man either, and would never consider him a good match for Cait. "Then you shall not marry him," Nicol assured her.

She heaved a sigh of relief. "We buried Edan beside Father and Mother. Nicol, shall you be our laird now?"

Nicol had not thought that far ahead yet, but he supposed he was and nodded.

"The people know not what to do, save what they have always done. They fear the Straiton shall bring their sheep and let them feast on our wheat. What shall we do?" She tipped her head to one side and looked up at him, "What best can we do?"

"I know not." Nicol admitted." With the others following, he urged his horse down a path that led to the back of the village. As soon as he reached another clump of trees with bushes high enough to give the horses good cover, he stopped and dismounted. "Cait, will you not wait with the horses?" He was relieved when she nodded.

As quietly as they could, the men crept through the bushes until they came to the foot of a high knoll. On their bellies, they crawled to the top and cautiously peered over. Below was a modest village, with three cottages that were now empty due to the winter deaths. Normally there would be fires in all the hearths as the night meal was being prepared, but not on the eve of this night. The lack of smoke drifting upward was a sure sign the entire clan was warning them not to come home.

Near a creek that ran behind the village was all that remained of a cottage built long ago, the wall stones of which had been used to build a new cottage. It was in that hearth that Logan lit the fire to caution them, and it was likely that fire they smelled. The hearth still smoldered, but now there was a Straiton standing guard not far away. His attendance no doubt prevented any of the captives from adding more fuel without arousing suspicion, particularly on such a hot night.

Lying next to Nicol, Murdock whispered, "The Straiton know not we are gone?"

"If not yet, they shall discover it soon enough," Nicol answered. His people looked so lost and defeated that it tugged at his heart. They were peaceful Scots and nothing so unthinkable as this had ever happened to them before. The women, Nicol noticed, gave the Straiton guards a wide berth as they walked past and went about their evening chores, as if they feared being snatched away. That morning, Nicol would have thought that impossible – now he feared for them as well.

The Straiton laird was not that much older than Edan, Adair Straiton having suffered the same winter illness as they, and the death of their leader. Under different circumstances the two new lairds might have been friends, but not now – now that Laird Straiton had exhibited the full extent of his greed for all to see.

However, Nicol and Adair were not, and could not ever be, friends. Their dislike for each other began the spring in which Nicol started his eighth year. Nicol's dog liked Adair not at all, growled when he came near, and on a particular occasion showed her teeth. Without a second thought, Adair loaded his bow, shot Nicol's dog and then killed all four of her pups. Nicol was furious and complained, but his father denied his request for revenge. Even so Nicol swore the day would come, for he had not forgotten. Yet as the years passed, the Straiton clan grew more quickly and became far greater in number, making them impossible to fight. Therefore, even Nicol strived to keep the peace, albeit an uneasy peace.

Once a good distance apart, the Straitons had expanded until the two villages were no longer separated but by the road, making it possible to see enough of their village to determine if they were preparing to fight. As far as Nicol could tell they were not and why would they be? Why fight when committing an outright swindle was far easier?

Nicol scooted over until he could see the wheat field. Situated on a strip of land far longer than it was wide, the men Nicol would soon begin to think of as his, were slowly wielding their scythes in an effort to cut the stalks so the wheat berries could be harvested, while the Straiton guards gladly looked on instead of helping.

"They have enslaved them," Nicol said under his breath.

For a very long time, Nicol, Murdock and Inek watched the people below in stunned silence, for it seemed unnatural that such could be possible. They watched as Murdock and Inek's mother, Elspeth, secretly hid a sword in the dirt behind her cottage and then went on her way as if nothing was amiss. Yet the children did not play or sing happy songs. Instead, they held fast to their mothers even though the mothers were put upon to push them away so the work could continue. As near as Nicol could tell, all but one of their milk cows had been taken away, and he could see no horses at all. Even if they had a place to go, the people were now condemned to walk.

He had seen enough. With a heavy heart he eased himself back down the knoll. He thought to fight them, even wanted to fight them, but it would prove nothing. He was taught and taught well, that some of the people had to survive no matter the price, for there was no other way to preserve the clan.

As soon as Murdock also began to quietly slide back down, Inek followed. "I shall see where they have taken the lads," Inek told Nicol.

"As shall I?" Murdock asked Nicol, instead of telling him the way his brother did.

It was to be Nicol's first command, which he gave with a simple nod. There was no need to caution them, for they knew the dangers as well as he did. He watched them head down a different path, one that would lead to the Straiton village, as soon as they were out of sight, he slipped back into the forest to see about his sister.

To his surprise, the horses were there, but Cait was gone. In a panic, he quickly glanced around. "Cait?" he asked more loudly than he intended. When she didn't answer, he looked for footprints in the dirt. Even then, he could not determine in which direction she had gone. "Cait?" he said again in a lower tone of voice.

"Over here."

"Where?" he asked trying to determine where the voice was coming from. Above the bushes to his right, Cait slowly raised her hand. He cautiously approached and when he was close enough, he peeked over the bush. She sat on the ground with her knees pulled up to her chin and her arms wrapped around her knees. Cait looked even more upset than she had been when he left her. "Cait, why do you hide?" he whispered.

"Cairn Straiton seeks me. We must get away with all due haste...afore he marries me!"

Nicol nearly chuckled, but he knew her well enough to know she would not enjoy his sense of humor just now. "Do you not know I am your laird now and I dinna, nor shall I ever, give my consent?" She agreed and was so relieved; she drew in a breath that made him wonder just how long she had been holding it. He walked around the bush and sat down beside her.

"Did Cairn find the horses?" he asked, still keeping his voice low.

"Nay, not yet, but I heard him call my name."

Nicol paused to listen, but he heard nothing and changed the subject. "Sister, I am in need of your help."

"Me? What could I possibly do?"

"I saw Elspeth bury a sword behind her cottage and I fear they shall try to fight before we get back. Can you not tell them to wait?"

"Wait for what?"

"Wait for us to find help and return."

Her eyes grew wider. "Why can you not tell them? Suppose Cairn..."

"Of course, if you be not brave enough."

Cait frowned, looked down, shifted her eyes left to right, and then released another huge breath. "Very well, I shall do it, but you must promise to rescue me should Cairn drag me off and try to marry me!"

"I give you my pledge. Tell them we shall light the hearth as a sign we have come back."

She started to get up, paused as though she had changed her mind, and then finally got to her feet. She glanced around to be sure it was safe, gathered her courage, and then headed through the woods toward the village.

Nicol let her get a little ahead of him and then followed.

Cait hid when she thought it necessary, and then continued on when it was safe. As luck would have it, Elspeth was washing clothing in the shallow part of a creek that ran outside the village. Acting casual, Cait said a greeting so as not to startle Elspeth, grabbed a shirt as though she had come to help, and then dipped it in the water. As she washed the shirt, and without looking at the Elspeth, she whispered the words her brother told her to say. As soon as Elspeth nodded her understanding, Cait handed her the wet shirt, and hurried back up the path.

She had not gone far before she spotted Nicol. When he motioned for her to come, she obediently followed him into a clump of nearby bushes. Soon, she knew why. The dreaded Cairn was yelling her name and he was definitely coming closer. She rolled her eyes, and crouched down as far as she could behind her brother.

To Nicol's delight, Cairn received an answer and it wasn't hard to guess who was calling him. "Cairn?" the squeaky pretend female voice called from several feet away. It worked and in no time at all, Cairn turned and headed for the voice. As soon as Cairn was gone, Nicol took Cait's hand and hurried her to the horses. He mounted his horse and then quickly pulled her up behind him. A moment later, Murdock and Inek arrived, got on their horses and followed Nicol away from the village. When he returned to the same shallow river they had crossed before, Nicol led them into the trees again to hide until they were certain they had not been followed.

They waited, listened and watched for movement in the foliage.

What they needed was fresh water, and time to decide what to do. Believing they had not been followed, Nicol motioned for them to return to the river. He helped his sister slide off the horse, dismounted and walked to the water. Next, he pulled a cloth out of his belt and dipped it in the shallow part of the river. In all the excitement, he'd hardly noticed the dampness until then. He washed his face, his neck and arms, rinsed the cloth and then stood up.

After the brothers cupped their hands and drank from the fresh water, Murdock was the first to speak, "They keep Logan and the others bolted in a cottage."

"We must go back," Inek insisted. "We must free them!"

"How?" Nicol asked. His question was answered by blank stares. "We must first gather warriors to help us."

Inek stood up and scoffed, "Where be these warriors?"

Nicol did not answer. Instead, he handed the wet cloth to his sister so she could wash. Still young enough, Cait's nose and cheeks held the freckles her long red hair demanded of most of the youngsters in her clan. Even so, she was old enough and was to be married soon. Now Hensen, the young man she told Nicol she fancied, was behind a bolted door in the Straiton cottage. Yet, it did not appear that Hensen was foremost on Cait's mind.

"'Twas just in jest," she blurted out. "Hensen and I tried to prevent Edan, but..."

Nicol put his arm around her, and tried to comfort her. "Shhhh. 'Twas not yours to prevent him."

A new round of tears rolled down her cheeks. "Yet, he was our brother and I loved him...even after he went daft."

"Aye, I loved him as well." His words did not seem to offer her much comfort, but she nodded her understanding anyway. When she began to tell what happened in more detail, he just let her talk, always mindful to listen for approaching horses or watch for movement in the forest. With no wind, movement in the forest would be easy to spot.

"Therefore, no one else died," Cait finally said.

"I'm pleased to hear that," said Inek.

At last, she took a deep breath and let go of her brother. Cait went to the water to wet the cloth again, and then washed her face and arms. As was the custom, Murdock and Inek stood guard, just as they would for any woman away from the village.

Nicol watched the thirsty horses drink from the river and then saw them wander down stream to a patch of tall grass alongside the creek. Murdock and Inek had become uncommonly quiet, but then, what was there to say? Still, he wondered if they would continue to follow him, or if they would break away and attempt to free the others without his say. After all, he had not yet truly become their laird. There were ceremonies and pledges to be had before it was ordained. Still, he could think of no one more honorable or loyal than Murdock and Inek, if not to him, to the clan.

They had known for weeks that Clan Straiton wanted their land. Before Nicol's father fell ill, Laird Straiton offered gold and silver for the land, but he was denied for the clan had worked that same land for generations and it was needed for the generations to come.

What the Straiton could not buy, they simply took and Nicol neglected to consider the possibilities of that happening. He was determined not to let it happen again. Nicol whistled a signal to the others and went to mount his horse. They had not rested the horses as long as they should have, but he was eager to put more distance between them and the Straiton.

"Where do we go?" Murdock asked as he lifted Cait up so she could ride again behind her brother. Murdock boasted of being their best hunter, easily beating all the other men in contests, and had even won a prize or two when the villages gathered for festivals. "Say again how we shall find these warriors?"

Nicol answered, while he waited for the others to get mounted. "There be a story of old, that claims a clan of Viking warriors hide in Scotland."

"Vikings?" Inek asked. "We've not seen a Viking in..."

"That we know of," Nicol added with an emphatic nod. "If the story be true, we must find them. We have no choice other."

"If the story be true," Inek scoffed. As a child, Inek was often teased for being the shortest, until he promised to break the neck of the next man who made fun of him. He could do it too, and no one doubted his word, for as a woodcutter, his biceps were larger than most.

Nicol was not in the mood for doubt. "Have you another idea?" His question was met with silence and eyes that turned down. "Good. We shall hunt and fish along the way, and when we meet a stranger, we shall ask."

Inek was still not convinced. "Ask what precisely?"

Not truly convinced either, Murdock snickered, "Ask if they know where the Vikings might be."

Inek rolled his eyes. "They shall think us daft."

Nicol said nothing more on that subject. It would be dark soon, so he led the way across the glen and up the hill on the other side. He grew up believing there were Vikings hidden in Scotland and he had no reason to doubt it.

(End of Sample Chapter)

Pick up your copy of Viking Valor, book 8 today.

More Marti Talbott Books

www.martitalbott.com

To discover free Marti Talbott books and more historical novels filled with castles and kings, love and war, triumph and tribulation - click here[1].

Follow Clan MacGreagor through multiple generations beginning with *The Viking*[2] where it all began, *The Highlanders*[3] and their struggle to survive, *Marblestone Mansion*[4] and the duke who simply could not get rid of his scandalous duchess, and still more historical stories in *The Lost MacGreagor Books*[5]. Then check out **Marti's contemporary romance/mysteries**[6] in *Missing Heiress, Greed and a Mistress, The Dead Letters*, and *The Locked Room*. Other books include the *Carson Series*[7], *Leanna, (a short story)*, and *Seattle Quake 9.2*[8].

Marti's Website[9] Talk to Marti on Facebook[10]

---

1. http://www.martitalbott.com

2. *http://www.martitalbott.com/viking-series*

3. *http://www.martitalbott.com/highlander-series*

4. *http://www.martitalbott.com/marblestone-mansion*

5. *http://www.martitalbott.com/The-Lost-MacGreagor-Books*

6. http://www.martitalbott.com/m-t-romance

7. *http://www.martitalbott.com/the-carson-series*

8. *http://www.martitalbott.com/more-marti-talbott-books*

9. http://www.martitalbott.com

10. https://www.facebook.com/marti.talbot

Don't miss out!

Visit the website below and you can sign up to receive emails whenever Marti Talbott publishes a new book. There's no charge and no obligation.

https://books2read.com/r/B-A-OYD-DHZS

BOOKS 2 READ

Connecting independent readers to independent writers.

Also by Marti Talbott

Marti Talbott's Highlander Series
Marti Talbott's Highlander Series 1
Marti Talbott's Highlander Series 2
Marti Talbott's Highlander Series 3
Marti Talbott's Highlander Series 4
Marti Talbott's Highlander Series 5
Betrothed
The Golden Sword, Book 7
Abducted, Book 8
A Time of Madness
Triplets
Secrets
Choices
Ill-Fated Love
The Other Side of the River
Marti Talbott's Highlander Omnibus, Books 1 - 3
Leanna: A Clean Highlander Short Story

Scandalous Duchess Series
Marblestone Mansion, Book 1
Marblestone Mansion, Book 2
Marblestone Mansion, Book 3

Marblestone Mansion, Book 4
Marblestone Mansion, Book 5
Marblestone Mansion, Book 6
Marblestone Mansion, Book 7
Marblestone Mansion, Book 8
Marblestone Mansion, Book 9
Marblestone Mansion, Book 10
Marblestone Mansion, (Omnibus, Books 1 - 3)

The Lost MacGreagor Books
Beloved Ruins, Book 1
Beloved Lies, Book 2
Beloved Secrets, Book 3
Beloved Vows, Book 4

The Viking Series
The Viking
The Viking's Daughter
The Viking's Son
The Viking's Bride
The Viking's Honor
Viking Blood
The Unwanted Bride
Viking Valor

Standalone
Seattle Quake 9.2
Suspects (The Botham/Miracle Murders)

Watch for more at www.martitalbott.com.